Reuben

Ellie's People · 5 ·

Books by
Mary Christner Borntrager

Ellie
Rebecca
Rachel
Daniel
Reuben
Andy
Polly
Sarah
Mandy
Annie

*Over half a million books in print
in the Ellie's People Series*

*This series is available
in regular type and
in large-print type.*

Reuben

Mary Christner Borntrager

HERALD PRESS
Scottdale, Pennsylvania
Waterloo, Ontario

Library of Congress Cataloging-in-Publication Data

Borntrager, Mary Christner, 1921-
    Reuben / Mary Christner Borntrager.
        p.   cm.—(Ellie's people ; 5)
        Summary: Growing up in a close-knit Amish family, Reuben
struggles with peer pressure and his desire to own a horse.
      ISBN 0-8361-3593-8 (alk. paper)
      ISBN 0-8361-3640-3 (large-print pbk.)
      [1. Amish—Fiction. 2. Mennonites—Fiction. 3. Peer
pressure—Fiction.] I. Title. II. Series: Borntrager, Mary
Christner, 1921-   Ellie's people ; 5.
PS3552.07544R4 1992
813'.54—dc20   92-5432
[Fic]

Scripture is from *The Holy Bible, King James Version.*

REUBEN
Copyright © 1992 by Herald Press, Scottdale, Pa. 15683
  Published simultaneously in Canada by Herald Press,
  Waterloo, Ont. N2L 6H7. All rights reserved
Library of Congress Catalog Card Number: 92-5432
International Standard Book Number: 0-8361-3593-8
Printed in the United States of America
Cover art by Edwin Wallace/Book design by Paula M. Johnson

09 08 07 06 05   10 9 8 7 6

49,500 copies in print in all editions

To order or request information, please call
1-800-759-4447 (individuals); 1-800-245-7894 (trade).
Web site: www.heraldpress.com

To my brothers,
Willis and Glenn,
who also worked horses

ELLIE'S PEOPLE

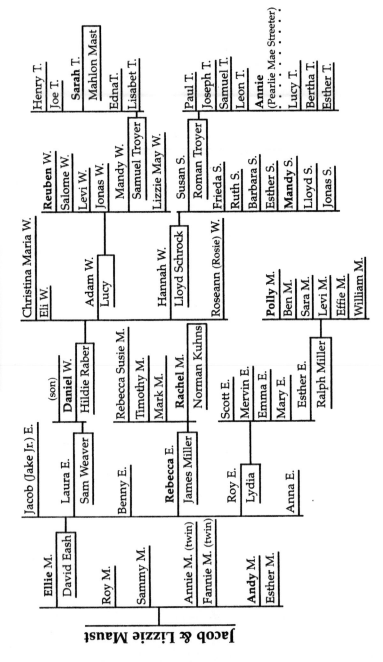

Contents

1
The Secret

"Come once, Reuben. Dad wants you to help white-wash the cow barn."

Startled by his sister's unexpected appearance in the buggy shed, Reuben quickly tried to conceal something behind his back.

"What's that you're hiding from me?" quizzed Salome.

"None of your business, *Melaasich Gsicht* (Molasses Face)," replied Reuben. "You stick worse than molasses."

"You'd better let me see, or I'll tell Dad. I bet it's something worldly we aren't allowed to have."

Reuben and Salome were Daniel Weaver's grandchildren. Their father was Adam, and their mother's name was Lucy. Reuben had two brothers, Levi and Jonas, and two more sisters completed the family, Lizzie Mae and Mandy.

Adam and his wife taught their children the Bible

and the way of Amish life. Any other lifestyle was considered worldly.

"If I tell you, will you keep it a secret?" bargained Reuben.

Even though Salome thought it might be something wicked, her curiosity got the better of her, and she promised.

"Forever and ever?" Reuben added, trying to stress the importance of her commitment.

"Yes, but *mach schnell* (hurry). Dad may come soon to see what keeps you."

"Here, then, look." Reuben produced a slick magazine with a picture of a horse and a fashionably dressed girl on the cover.

"*Ach* (oh), such a book!" his sister exclaimed.

"Mind now, you promised not to tell."

It had been raining that morning, so there was no field work to do. Reuben slipped the magazine inside some wrapping paper and put it under his shirt. He went upstairs to change into dry clothes.

Once more he yielded to the urge to look at the magazine Willy had loaned him. He became so engrossed in its contents that time slipped by.

The Weaver children did not get to see many books. "Too much dreaming you do *mit Bicher* (with books)," his father had declared. Adam Weaver wanted his family to learn that life is real, not just made of dreams. He wanted to make sure his children learned to work.

"What's been keeping you, Reuben?" he asked as his son finally stepped inside the stable.

"I guess this gentle rain just made me a little poky, and I lost track of the time," Reuben replied lamely.

"Maybe this will speed you up," said Adam. "If we get our work finished by noon, I plan to drive into town for some lumber. How would you like to ride along?"

"Sure, Dad, I'd like that fine."

Adam knew his son loved horses, and any chance to drive one was a real treat. Reuben began to work with a will. He wondered which horse they would take. He liked them all, but Star was his favorite. She was newly broken to the buggy, and full of pep and vigor.

"May we take Star this afternoon?"

"Oh, I don't believe we'd better," answered his dad. "We have to bring home some two-by-fours, so we need to take the *Wagge* (spring wagon)." The spring wagon had only one seat in the front and an open box extending out over the back wheels.

"I can't imagine Star being gentle enough to bring anything home in one piece in the *Wagge*," Adam chuckled.

Reuben himself smiled at the thought of it. Then he remembered the horse in the magazine he had hidden upstairs. What a horse that one was! *Some day I'm going to have one just like him,* Reuben decided. *Some day.*

"Are you dreaming again?" His dad's voice startled him. "You're just standing there with your dripping brush. It looks as if you were hundreds of miles away, staring at nothing. What were you thinking about this time?"

"Just stuff," Reuben replied as he began swinging his brush rapidly, splattering whitewash around as he stroked it on the stable partitions. The whitewash looked like white paint, only it was much thinner.

"Whoa! Slow down. I want to get the job done, but I hadn't planned on whitewashing the floor of the cow barn."

"I'll be more careful, Dad," Reuben promised.

"See that you are," Adam counseled.

His son couldn't understand why the cow stable had to be all cleaned up just because the Jake Maust reunion was to be at the Weaver home this year.

"You know our *Weibsleit* (women folk)," Adam reminded him. "They want everything all spiffed up. Jake and Lizzie Maust's descendants have grown to a large number. Lucy thinks the house is too small for so many, and we may need to set up in the feedway of the barn. You can figure out the rest." His dad grinned as he winked at him.

Reuben was satisfied to be Amish. He loved family get-togethers and the importance they felt at handing down their traditions and heritage. Reuben remembered the stories his grandfather Daniel told about his own grandmother Ellie, the daughter of Jake and Lizzie Maust.

There were other tales, too, such as the one about how Reuben's grandmother, Hildie, had disappeared when his dad, Adam, was a child. And how his grandpa's first cousin Rachel had grown up in a Mennonite family and then went to live with her Amish grandmother Ellie, became Amish, and married Norman Kuhns.

Reuben was glad his people were close-knit, with love for God and time to visit with neighbors. He had a feeling of security in knowing that they took care of each other and rarely needed prisons, divorce courts, children's homes, or welfare systems.

As Reuben's family visited in other Amish homes, he noticed that the grandparents often lived in a small *Dawdy Haus* (grandparents' house) connected to the larger farmhouse. Thus they could see some of their children and grandchildren every day and pass on the family stories.

"That's it," Adam announced. "You can coat that last door while I harness the horses and hitch them to the *Wagge*. Put the rest of the whitewash away and rinse out the empty buckets."

"*Ya* (yes), Dad, I'll be right with you," Reuben replied as he rushed to finish. He wanted to help get the horses out.

Like other Amish children, Reuben was taught to work, share responsibility, and be respectful. His dad said that would build strong character. Reuben actually liked to work, especially with others. It made him feel needed and a part of the family.

Yet Reuben knew their Amish people were not perfect. Many times his parents taught their children, "We must not only read the Bible; we must live it."

Most of all, Reuben enjoyed doing projects alongside his father. Adam seldom spoke harshly to his children. Reuben admired and appreciated him for this. Unlike Willy Chupp's father, Adam was kind and gentle, yet firm.

Perhaps, thought Reuben, *Willy is so unruly because his dad isn't nice to him.* After Sunday service, held every two weeks, most of the boys made *Schpott* (fun) of Willy. They even nicknamed him *Wooly*. Some said it suited him just right because he was wild and a fighter.

Reuben's parents told their children to be nice to Willy and befriend him, but not to follow his ways. That, however, turned out to be a problem for Reuben. He didn't mean to do the mischief Willy was always proposing. Yet when they were together, somehow it just happened.

Willy had interesting ideas for pranks and many wild exploits to brag about. Reuben never was sure at times whether Willy was telling the truth.

What would Reuben's parents say if they saw the magazine Willy had slipped to Reuben after school?

They must never know. He would give it back to Willy the first chance he got. It really wasn't bad. There were pictures of horses and fancy *englisch* (non-Amish) girls with painted faces, and some articles about breaking and training horses.

Then why do I feel so guilty that I hide the magazine? Reuben questioned himself. His parents might not object to the horses, but the *englisch* girls would be forbidden.

Why, oh, why did my sister have to catch me with that magazine? Yet she had promised to keep the secret. Reuben sincerely hoped she would.

2

Dozens of Cousins

Saturday morning dawned bright and sunny. The day of the reunion finally arrived, and with it came many cars, vans, and buggies winding their way to the Adam Weaver farm.

"Reuben, you and Levi help unhitch the horses and show the men where they can tie them by the hay wagons," Adam instructed his sons. "Jonas, make sure you have enough chalk to number the buggies." Since the buggies were similar, they would number them to avoid a mix-up.

Reuben was glad to help with the horses. Nothing could have pleased him more.

"I'll be busy setting up tables and benches on the lawn," Adam stated.

"Dad," said Reuben, "I like to help with the horses, but I won't know a lot of the people who come to reunions."

"Well, that's part of the reason we have them, so you

will get to know all your cousins and other relatives," his father explained. "Be friendly, and you'll find it's easy to become *bekannt* (acquainted). Hurry now! The first buggies are coming down the driveway."

Lucy was busy, too, flitting here and there, making sure everything was in order. It was quite a feat to arrange so many things for such a large gathering.

"Lizzie Mae, you and Mandy carry the big tin tub out under the maple tree by the spring house," Lucy directed. "Help each other fill it with water for washing up. I'll send Salome out with towels and soap. Ach, I need a soap dish and something to lay the towels on. I thought we were ready, but there are always last-minute things."

Her daughters tried to think of some way to make things easier for their mother. "Mom," suggested Lizzie Mae, "Reuben could carry the milk bench from the barn, and we could use that." The milk bench was a stand on which to set the full milk pails out of hungry cats' reach during milking time.

"*Ya*, please ask him to set the milk bench at the spring house," agreed Lucy, "and *mach schnell* (hurry). Some cousins are here already."

Lizzie Mae ran to tell Reuben at once. He didn't like the interference, but nevertheless he obeyed. After he set the bench where it was needed, he rushed back to the front drive to be ready to take charge of the rigs as relatives arrived.

Reuben looked over every horse he helped unhitch and compared it to the one he had seen in the magazine. *None can measure up to him*, Reuben thought. *He is a prince among horses. That's what I'll name my horse when*

16

I get one—Prince. He'll be just like my secret horse. His mind was wandering from the job at hand.

"*Was* (what)?" Reuben exclaimed with a start.

"I just asked for the third time, where am I to put my horse?" said a newcomer.

"Ach," replied Reuben. "I guess I didn't hear you. Lead her behind the buggy shed and through the pasture gate. There are several flat wagons there with hay. Most of the place is shaded. I'm sorry I didn't hear you."

"That's alright," the stranger commented. "I've got boys, too, and they daydream sometimes."

Then with a chuckle he added, "I'm Dan Nisly, an uncle to your dad. You look a lot like your father. He used to daydream when he was a boy. We teased him about always thinking of *schnee Meed* (pretty girls). You are a bit too young for that, though, I'd say." He chuckled again as he started for the pasture gate.

Reuben's face felt hot and flushed. He decided right then that he didn't care for Dan Nisly. But he soon forgot about that encounter as the flood of people kept coming. Eventually he and Levi counted and marked thirty-eight buggies. They had to get some more hay out of the barn for the horses.

The girls who came that day mostly stood in groups whispering, giggling, or holding *Bobblin* (babies). The boys were also clustered together, watching the food being set out, and jostling each other a bit. They would let the real wrestling and play for the afternoon.

They all were hungry, and it was time to eat. The tables were laden with so many different tempting dishes, one scarcely knew where to begin. The people were chattering and laughing so much that it was hard to get everyone's attention. Adam finally succeeded by banging two cooking pot lids together.

"Before we eat we will ask our oldest member to say a few words and call us to prayer. Then we can file by both sides of the table and serve ourselves. After we have eaten, we ask that you get your families together so we can all find out where you belong and where you're from.

"After the introductions, great-grandpa Eash requests that we sing awhile. You may then be free to visit, pitch horseshoes, play ball, or whatever. That is, if we can still stand on our feet after all this food has been taken care of."

Adam's last remark naturally brought some laughter, and one cousin interrupted: "Don't worry, we'll all do our part with the food."

"I'm sure you will," gibed another cousin.

"There'll be enough food for everyone," Adam assured them. "So now let's give thanks."

Great-grandpa David rose to his feet and steadied himself with a homemade cane. He smiled at his wife, Ellie, and with a quavery voice remarkably strong for one his age, he expressed gratitude for each one present, and especially for those who had come from a distance. "What a large family we have become! Let us thank God for his many blessings."

They paused for a period of silent prayer, and even with so many restless youngsters and fussy babies waiting to be fed, it was surprisingly quiet. Finally David pronounced the "Amen," and the feasting began.

As people began to fill their plates and find a seat, the volume of sound built up once more. Men and boys ate first, as usual. The women kept filling the serving dishes as the men emptied them.

They were farmers, carpenters, and craftsmen used to manual work, and they had hearty appetites. The assortment of pies was a big attraction. Many took second servings, but even so, there was food left after everyone was satisfied.

Reuben never knew he had so many relatives. They had come to Ohio from Indiana, Illinois, Iowa, Kansas, New York, Pennsylvania, and even Ontario. Although they all talked *Deitsch* (Pennsylvania German), their accents varied a bit depending on where they were from.

After the introductions and the singing, the older folks sat on chairs in the shade and visited. There were enough boys for several ball teams. Pitching horseshoes caught the young men's fancy. Here and there a friendly wrestling match broke out on the grass in response to some bragging or test-of-strength challenges. The girls stood around watching the ball games, whispering, and giggling some more.

Reuben thought the girls were silly. In fact, they reminded him of a gaggle of geese. He caught sight of his sister, Salome, talking to a girl he had never seen before. What were they talking about? The girl looked shocked, and Reuben worried that Salome had told his secret.

The day ended too soon, it seemed. The numbering system worked for the buggies. Reuben and Levi watered the horses and helped each family get on their way. Suddenly everyone was gone.

Reuben watched for a chance to talk to his sister alone. At chore time when she was feeding the hens, he had the opportunity.

"Did you tell?" he asked.

"Tell what?" Salome wondered.

"You know, about the book."

"Of course not," she assured her brother.

"Well, you'd better not."

"Why would I want to tell it, anyway?"

"I'm going to give it back, so just don't say anything."

"I won't," she promised again.

Everyone was tired and ready for bed, but what a day they had enjoyed! As Reuben fell asleep, he had visions of dozens of cousins petting his beautiful dream horse.

3

Cat's-Eyes and Aggies

"Adam," announced Lucy, "I've invited Roman Chupps and Freeman Wengerds for dinner next Sunday, so I'll need to go into town for a few things. Can you take me there?"

"Well, I really don't have time to go along, but maybe Reuben can," her husband answered. "He always likes to drive any horse."

"The girls and I could go alone, only sometimes we have to carry the groceries so far. If the hitching rack is full, then we end up tying our rig at the feed mill. That's way on the south side of town."

Reuben was happy at the prospect of going to town. He knew his mother would let him drive, and a buggy horse would move faster than the plodding workhorses he usually drove.

"May we take Star?" he asked his dad.

Without waiting for an answer, he added, "I know I could handle her, Dad."

"*Ach du lieber, nee* (oh, my land, no)!" exclaimed Lucy. "She goes so fast and shies at every car, plus lots of other things along the way."

"Ach, Mom," protested Reuben, "you don't need to worry. I can handle her."

To the relief of his wife, Adam settled the matter. "No, Reuben, you'll take Mol. She's safe and reliable. Your mom will enjoy her trip to town more that way, and you'll be safer."

"If we ever get there," Reuben muttered. "Mol is so slow, it'll take a long time."

"Better to be slow and safe than go so fast and have an upset," cautioned Mother.

Adam helped Reuben harness and hitch up Mol to the buggy, and they started out. Just as Reuben had predicted, the trip to town was a slow and uneventful one.

Once more, to break the monotony, Reuben began to use his imagination. It was not easy to pretend Mol was his picture-book horse.

If this were his horse, Prince, they would be flying along with his hooves pounding like so many drumbeats. The wind would sound like rushing water. He could see the rippling muscles under his shining coat and his tail flying out behind.

Then his mother's voice brought him back to reality as they finally reached town.

"Reuben," she suggested, "while I go to the grocery, maybe you could go to the hardware store and get a new handle for my broken hoe. The hoe is in the back buggy box. They don't seem to make things to last anymore. Here is some money to pay the bill."

They were fortunate to find space at the hitching post. Reuben tied Mol, took the broken hoe, and headed for the hardware.

Other Amish boys would stop and admire the fancy cars parked along the curbs, but that was never a temptation for Reuben. Cars were noisy, and besides, the bishop and his dad said they were worldly.

Sometimes, though, if one had to travel too far for a horse, then he guessed it made sense to use a car or a van. Only twice had he ridden in one, and he had felt rather naughty until his dad explained that it's alright in time of need.

He had the hoe handle replaced and was back at the buggy in good time. Then he made his way to the grocery, where his mother was just finishing her purchases, and gave her the change from the transaction at the hardware.

Reuben willingly picked up the heavier bags for his mother and lugged them to the buggy. He stashed them securely in the box behind the seat.

"Reuben," said Lucy Weaver, "you have been such a good help. I bought a little something for each of the other children today. You didn't talk back or make a big fuss about driving Mol instead of Star. I'll let you choose something for yourself.

"But mind, now, it shouldn't cost more than a quarter. That's what I spent for the other children, and you know I need to be fair."

"I know what I want," Reuben replied without hesitating.

"Whatever could it be?" asked Lucy, sensing his excitement.

"At the hardware store I saw some marbles. They are really nice. If I could get them today, then on Sunday Willy and I could play marbles."

"Do you know how much they cost?" his mother asked.

"No, I didn't check. But, Mom, you just ought to see them!"

"Well, if we hurry, we can go and find out what the price is for those marbles."

Reuben led his mother to the showcase where the beauties were displayed. They were nice, sparkling in the store lights, Lucy had to admit, but they cost forty-five cents.

"Reuben, that's more than I paid for the other gifts. What will the others say?"

Seeing how crestfallen her son looked and considering what an obedient boy he was, Lucy reconsidered. "Well, if you let your brothers and sisters play with them and do some extra chores around home, I may buy them for you."

"Oh, *ich duh* (I'll do it)," Reuben promised. "I sure will."

"Extra chores may mean cleaning the chicken house and the cistern. You don't like either of those jobs."

Reuben looked once more at that bag of marbles and hesitated as though weighing the choices. But the sight of those colorful cat's-eyes, aggies, and boulders was too tempting. The marbles won out.

"I'll do it, Mom," he promised as he reached for the bag.

"You won't complain when asked to do those dirty chores?"

"I'll try not to."

"That's good enough for me," Lucy told her son. "Come, it's time we go. Soon it'll get dark."

"Ya," said Reuben, clutching his package tightly and grinning happily.

Bought toys for Amish children were a rare treat. Therefore, they were especially treasured and well cared for. Mandy and Lizzie Mae each received a candy dish, and Levi and Jonas were given puzzles. How delighted they were!

Reuben could hardly wait until the coming of Sunday and their company. He was glad they had every other Sunday to spend visiting with friends and relatives. Reuben liked to go to church in homes, but without doubt he enjoyed the big company dinners on the "between Sundays," the alternate Sundays when services were not held.

Soon after Roman Chupps and Freeman Wengerds arrived, Reuben brought out his marbles. Both Willy Chupp and Reuben held them up to the light and admired them.

"Let's play for keeps," proposed Willy.

"Oh no," responded Reuben, "I couldn't do that. I just got these. Mom bought them for me. They're brand new, and I am supposed to save them for my brothers and sisters to play with, too."

"I say if I hit any of your marbles, then they're mine," Willy defiantly informed him. He had chosen his largest boulder for a shooter.

Willy was an excitable boy, and Reuben didn't know what to do. But Willy's father saw the conflict and took charge.

"Willy, you play fair now," he warned his son. "Remember, you're Reuben's guest."

But then the adults became engrossed in their conversations and didn't pay attention to the boys. As they played, Willy got Reuben's nicest aggies and two blue cat's-eyes.

"If you don't let me keep them," whispered Willy, "I'll tell about the magazine I loaned you and say it's yours."

He wouldn't, thought Reuben, *or would he?*

4
For Keeps

Reuben watched as Willy slyly put the marbles he claimed into the two large pockets on his homemade *Hosse* (trousers).

Such pockets were made to carry pocketknives, handkerchiefs, and useful items, but they were often filled with things that caused mothers to squirm. Pockets would also hold marbles as well as insects, dead or alive, and large rubber bands for making slingshots. Women were careful when emptying the contents of the boys' *Hosse* before washing them.

"*Kummt esse* (come, eat)," called Lucy.

"Don't move the marbles," Willy instructed Reuben as though they belonged to him. "I've got five of yours already. We'll finish the game after lunch."

"I thought we'd go outdoors after we've eaten and start some games that everyone can play," Reuben suggested.

"Oh no," demanded Willy. "We're going to finish

this game. We'll keep shooting until I've got all the marbles."

Reuben did not answer. He knew there always had to be trouble when Willy was around. And especially since he was losing his marbles, Reuben was disgusted that Willy didn't obey his dad.

Lucy assigned each one a place at the table, beginning with Adam. He was the head of the household and was served first, after a silent prayer.

Reuben loved to listen to the men talk. Their conversation was mostly about crops, milk and grain prices, and horses. At the mention of horses, Reuben sat up and took notice.

That's how the upset happened. Turning to hear Freeman Wengerd tell about a nice trotter he bought, Reuben accidentally nudged Willy's arm with his elbow.

"*Nau guck was du mich gemacht hast duh* (now look what you made me do)!" Willy screamed in a voice an octave higher than normal.

Willy had just raised his glass for a sip of water, and the light jolt from Reuben's arm sent glass and water everywhere.

"You did it on purpose," Willy accused him.

"I didn't mean to," Reuben replied. "Really I didn't. I'm sorry."

"Like fun," Willy mocked. He would have continued his tantrum, but his father settled him.

"That's enough, Willy."

Willy slouched down in his chair.

"The women are cleaning everything up now, so just forget it."

"No, I won't," huffed Willy. "Every time Reuben hears the word *horse*, he goes wild."

"I said *genunk* (enough)!" bellowed Roman Chupp.

Reuben could hear Willy still mumbling, but only made out one word—*Bichli* (small book). That sent a shiver of fear into Reuben's heart. He would return that magazine to Willy this very day—and give up the picture of his beautiful wished-for horse.

He told himself that it wasn't right to hide something from his parents. He felt better already, knowing he would do right. God was watching all the time and knew he had that book. Anyhow, the picture of that horse was fixed so vividly in his mind that he didn't need the book anymore.

Reuben noticed how Willy's mother and brothers and sisters were ashamed because of his misbehavior. After the meal, Willy was complaining because his clothes and hair were still wet.

"You're about Reuben's size. Would you like to change into some of his clothes?" offered Lucy Weaver. "I'll hang these to dry in the sun. Reuben can show you where to change, and I'll give you a towel to dry your hair."

"No," moped Willy.

"Well then," his dad declared, "maybe we should hang you on the clothesline to dry out."

Several of the children burst out laughing at the thought of it.

Willy, however, pouted all the more.

After lunch Willy made his way to the living room to finish the marble game. To everyone's amazement, the marbles were scattered everywhere.

"Who did this?" shouted Willy.

"I don't know," Reuben answered. "I'm just as surprised as you are."

"I don't believe it. You sent someone in here to mess up our game because I was winning."

"No, I didn't. You know I was at the table all the time, and so were all the others."

At that moment Willy's little sister came toddling from behind a rocker with marbles in both hands.

"So it was you!" barked Willy, slapping his baby sister. "You get into everything, you dummy."

Baby Elsie started to cry. Mrs. Chupp tried to comfort her daughter. She sent one of her other children to fetch her husband to take care of Willy—again!

"Pick up every one of those marbles," Roman commanded his son, "and then you will spend the rest of the day with me. No more play. If you can't behave, then you'll just have to take your medicine."

Reuben didn't know what kind of medicine Roman Chupp referred to. Later his own father told him that meant punishment.

Throughout the afternoon, the other children enjoyed prisoner's base, hide-and-seek, no bears out tonight, and various games. Willy's brothers and sisters seemed really nice and were fun to play with.

Meanwhile, Willy sulked as he sat on the porch steps near the men and watched the youngsters having fun in the yard. Reuben waved to him several times, but he just turned and looked the other way.

Before it was time for the company to leave, Reuben slipped away to his upstairs room for one last look at his horse. Carefully he wrapped the magazine in paper and carried it downstairs under his shirt to return it to its rightful owner.

Willy was still angry and refused to take it. Reuben spied two empty gunnysacks in the back buggy box of Roman's rig. He quickly placed the magazine under those bags without anyone noticing. There! He felt better.

"You must come and visit us soon," suggested Mrs. Chupp and Mrs. Wengerd as they walked out to their buggies.

"Ya," added Mr. Wengerd. "It's your turn."

"Ach, who goes by turns?" laughed Adam.

That evening after chores, Reuben's parents reminisced over the day's happenings.

"I sure feel sorry for Roman Chupps," Lucy Weaver told her husband. "No wonder they don't get invited out more."

"Yes, I agree," responded Adam. "The way Willy acts—ei-yi-yi-yi! It makes me wonder so if he can't help it, or if he does it for mean."

"Willy told me once that he sometimes gets his own way if he acts up," Reuben informed them.

"Well, it's plain to see he didn't get the gentlest treatment from his dad," observed Adam. "Did you see how Roman jerked him around and pulled his ears?"

"Yes, I did," Lucy replied.

Reuben, too, felt sorry for Willy in a way.

"Have you seen my marbles, *Melaasich Gsicht?*" Reuben asked his sister.

"No," Salome answered. "And stop calling me *Melaasich Gsicht.*"

"He calls you that because he thinks you're sweet," teased Levi.

"Mom, have you seen my marbles?"

"No, Reuben, I haven't. Roman told Willy to pick them up, but I didn't see what he did with them."

I hope Willy will tell me what he did with them, Reuben thought as he made his way to bed that night.

5
They Fell into My Pocket

Summer went by quickly, and soon it was time for school once more.

"What did you pack in my lunch today?" Reuben asked Salome as they went out the drive toward the road.

"*Lattwarick Brot un kalti Wascht* (apple butter bread and cold sausage), and of course, half-moon pie," his sister replied.

"Well, I guess it will taste mighty good at lunchtime. Anyway, I'll be good and hungry after we win the ball game at first recess."

"How do you know you'll win?"

"Oh, who couldn't beat those fourth-grade babies?" Reuben twirled his arm and lunch box like a propeller to accent his boasting.

"Mom says you shouldn't call other people names," Salome reminded him. "Anyhow, you're in fifth grade, and that's only one higher."

"Mom doesn't need to know if you don't tell, *Melaasich Gsicht*."

"There, see, you did it again," Salome protested.

"Well, you stick to me like molasses. Why don't you walk with Levi and Jonas sometimes?"

"They're too poky. Besides, if I'm with you, I'm not afraid of Swartz's dog when we pass their place."

"Ach, he is all bark and no bite," Reuben told her.

"Well, anyway, I want to walk with you until we get by their house."

"Alright, but mind you don't tattle to Mom about me," Reuben bargained.

"Well, I didn't tell about the magazine with those pictures of the *englisch* girls and the horses, did I? But why do you want to do bad stuff?"

"I'm not doing bad stuff," Reuben defended himself. "I gave that magazine back to Willy." He kicked up little puffs of dust as they walked.

"You did!" exclaimed Salome, and then she added, "I'm glad. It made me feel bad to keep a secret and know you were hiding a worldly thing."

After they left the Swartz place and the barking dog behind, Salome skipped along to join other Amish girls coming out farm lanes and heading down the winding road for the one-room schoolhouse.

As they greeted their friends, the girls admired each other's new dresses. Made over the same pattern, the colors were of the darker shades, mostly brown, blue, green, and gray.

The dresses reached nearly to the ankles and were fastened in the back with a neat row of dark buttons from the neck to the waistline. Contrary to the fashions of the world, these young lassies counted it a joy to look alike. Mom said Salome's dresses must be long with a big hem to be let out so they would last all school year.

"She grows so fast," remarked Lucy.

Lizzie Mae and Mandy didn't go to school yet, but after Salome outgrew her dresses and aprons, they would be handed down to her sisters.

The boys talked baseball as they walked along. They planned their strategy until they reached the school yard. "We'll lay those third and fourth graders in the dust," bragged Reuben.

Salome heard him and wished he wouldn't talk so smart. She was in the third grade herself and felt loyal to her classmates. There were three boys and two girls in the third grade, and four boys and three girls in grade four. Fifth and sixth grades together had eight boys and six girls. It took the boys from two grades to make up one team.

Teacher John Zook welcomed each student and told them to find seats. Later he would assign places as he deemed best. This was his third year of teaching at Fir Hill School. Before then the school always employed an older girl. That worked fine for the younger pupils, but it became more than she could manage with older ones and all eight grades.

John was a strict teacher but a fair one. He never played favorites. The children liked him and generally obeyed.

"Well, I see I have more students this year," John remarked. "That's good. I remember you older ones, but I need the names of newcomers."

Some of the first-grade children were scared and a few tears rolled down their cheeks. Fortunately, the older girls who knew them were able to calm their fears. These families lived in the same neighborhood and attended the same church. Therefore, the smaller children had often been with these girls and trusted them. Later in the year the girls would help them with lessons.

At the first recess, the children agreed that Reuben and Floyd Yoder would be captains of the ball teams. They guessed numbers to see who would choose first. Two boys huddled and decided on a number, and the captain closest to guessing the right number began the selection process.

"We have a number between one and twenty," Jonas Hershberger told them.

"I pick number eighteen," Floyd declared.

"What do you choose, Reuben?" asked Eli Miller.

"How about number five?" ventured Reuben.

"You've got it, Reuben. It was seven."

"You'd better pick me first," Willy Chupp whispered in Reuben's ear. "If you don't, I'll tell about you-know-what!"

To avoid precious time and conflict, Reuben did select Willy. He couldn't deny that Willy was a good player, but he didn't like his attitude. The fifth and sixth graders won that game, but they had to struggle for it. The boys in third and fourth grade had some good players also.

"Just wait till noon recess," bragged Cristy Glick. "We'll show you how to play ball."

But to the disappointment of all, before noon

arrived, rain was coming down in sheets.

"This will put a stop to playing outdoors," announced Teacher John. "I have some quiet games you may use inside."

He provided them with fig mill, Uno, Dutch Blitz, Monopoly, Bible Travelogue, and, for the younger ones, a game of Candy Land and some easy puzzles.

"If only I could find my marbles," mused Reuben. "We could play marbles in the outside aisle. You never did tell me where you put them, Willy."

"So!" remarked Willy. "I picked them up. Hunt for them. I'm not coming over to get them for you."

Reuben wanted to remind him that he had them last, but to avoid an argument he remained silent. Little did he know what would take place that very evening.

After school, the children went straight home and did their chores before supper. After Reuben and the younger ones were sent to bed, their parents were sitting at the kitchen table. In the lamplight, Adam was reading out loud from *The Budget*, and Lucy was listening, darning socks, and commenting on the newsy letters from other Amish settlements.

Suddenly they heard their watchdog barking.

"Who could be coming at this hour?" Lucy asked her husband.

"I can't imagine," responded Adam, peering out the window as the dim lights of a buggy bobbed up and down in the darkness.

The Amish seldom knock, counting their neighbors as family. Soon the door opened, and in walked Roman Chupp with his son.

"*Wie geht's* (how do you do), Roman?" Adam greeted his friend. "What brings you out tonight?"

"I think I'll let Willy tell you," Roman answered.

"Marbles," said Willy, holding out a bulging paper bag. "They just fell into my pocket."

"Now, Willy, tell the truth," Roman demanded harshly.

Willy's lower lip shot out, and in a voice barely audible, he mumbled, "I took them."

"Go out and wait for me in the buggy," Roman ordered, giving his son a shove.

Reuben was asleep and heard none of this, but in the morning he was glad to have the marbles back. Later his father revealed the mystery and told him how the lost was found.

"Never steal, Reuben, and never hide the truth," Adam admonished his son.

Reuben felt a twinge of guilt. Should he tell of the magazine he had kept hidden?

6
Stilts and Fences

Reuben felt like he was ten feet tall. That's because he was walking on stilts.

The stilts were made from two narrow boards about six feet long. At the two-foot level, a short piece of wood was attached with screws crosswise on each stilt, and a leather strap was provided to hold one's toes in place. With these stilts he was taking giant steps.

It took real ingenuity and balance to master the art of stilt walking. Reuben could handle himself well on this contraption. Many times he ran, hopped, and even stepped over low fences.

"Let me try," begged Salome after watching her brother.

"Oh no, *Melaasich Gsicht*, I don't think you should," Reuben told her.

"But I know I can. It looks easy."

"It may look easy, but it isn't. You have to keep your balance and watch where you're going."

"You never let me do anything that's fun," Salome pouted.

"I just don't want you to get hurt."

"I won't get hurt. Please let me try."

"Well, come here then, but I'm going to hold on to you so you won't fall."

"Ach, you think I'm a *Bobbli* (baby). Well, I'm not."

"Okay, come here, and I'll help you up." Reuben placed the stilts against the side of the buggy shed.

"You always put the stilts up against a solid wall. That gives you support to get started and find your balance. Now, put one foot up under the leather strap and rest it on the crosspiece. Next, hop up with the other foot. Whoa! Why do you *schiddle* (shake) so? Are you scared?"

"No," declared Salome, but her trembling voice wasn't convincing.

"Alright, take another step, just like you do when you're walking."

Slowly and with unsteady movements, Salome began walking. If Reuben hadn't been there to steady her and talk her through the tryout, she would have fallen with her first step. Gradually she began to relax. Her confidence increased.

"Let go now, Reuben," she insisted.

"Not yet. You aren't ready to walk alone."

Salome had a determination and a mind of her own. She lurched forward to break free from Reuben, who lost his grip. Down she fell, face forward right into the gravel. She began screaming, and this brought Mother from her work in the kitchen.

"*Was is letz* (what's wrong)?" she asked Reuben.

"Salome wanted me to help her walk on the stilts. Then she tried to break away from me and walk on her own, and she fell."

"He didn't hold on to me. He pushed me," sobbed Salome.

"Reuben, did you push her?" asked Lucy.

"No, Mom, I didn't. I just lost my hold on her."

"Did so push me," Salome insisted.

Reuben couldn't believe his sister would tell the *Unwaahrheit* (untruth). It hurt him deeply.

"Well, let's get you to the house and clean up that face. You even have dirt and gravel in your hair. Reuben, until Dad gets back from town, I want you to weed the potatoes in the truck patch."

Reuben used to wonder why they called that large garden a truck patch. One day his father explained to him that it was because they raised extra vegetables there for their *englisch* neighbor Joe Erkel to haul by truck to market.

As Reuben made his way through the rows of potatoes, he thought about his sister's behavior. Why would Salome lie about what happened? As long as he could remember, they had been taught the importance of telling the truth. That was one of the Ten Commandments from the Bible. Reuben knew it well: "Thou shalt not bear false witness."

As he began to weed, he decided to hide his stilts and try not to use them when his sister was around. *That's hard to do, though,* he reasoned. *She's such a Molasses Face.*

Adam had a talk with his children that evening. He stressed the need to always be truthful. "You can't both be right, you know. I can't tell what happened today because I wasn't there. But you two know, and there is one more who knows. He is always with us.

"It grieves me that one of you is lying, but it grieves God more. Do you want to go to sleep tonight, knowing that you did wrong?"

Salome burst into tears. She ran to her mother, hid her face in her mother's apron, and sobbed.

"Reuben didn't push me. I fell. He didn't, and I said he did."

"I thought as much," responded Adam. "Do you have something to say to Reuben?"

"I'm sorry. I shouldn't have said you pushed me."

"I'm glad you told the truth, Salome. Now we will both feel better."

Since Reuben called her "Salome" and not "Molasses Face," she knew everything was alright.

"Maybe someday we'll try the stilts again," Reuben offered.

The other Weaver children, although younger, had witnessed this confession and forgiveness between their brother and sister. Adam and Lucy felt it was a good experience for them and a help to set their feet on the right path.

With this reconciliation, they were able to go to bed and sleep soundly.

Reuben, however, did have a habit of showing off with those stilts. One Sunday afternoon Willy Chupp's family came visiting again. Willy could handle the stilts, but not as well as Reuben.

"Bet I can do anything on those things you can," Willy boasted.

"No, you can't."

"Can so. Just tell the best trick you can do, and I bet I can do it better."

"No," said Reuben. He knew Willy was a daring fellow, and he didn't want to see him get hurt.

"See there. You know I can beat you at anything, so you won't tell me. *Du bist gehl* (you're yellow)," Willy taunted.

This was more than Reuben could take. "I'd just like to see you step over the pasture fence."

"That's nothing," mocked Willy.

"It has only one strand of barbed wire. I've done it often," Reuben coolly assured him.

Willy hesitated a moment.

"What're you waiting for?" asked Reuben.

Then against his better judgment, he added, "I dare you. I double dare you."

Willy began high-stepping toward the fence. He swung one leg across, but the rest of his body didn't make it. Down he came with his face and right hand on the barbed wire.

Willy was scratched and bleeding, and he yelled out in pain.

Right away Reuben knew this was big trouble. He didn't want his parents to know he had dared Willy. He decided to tell them he tried to discourage Willy from doing tricks. After all, that was true at first.

"I'm telling on you," shouted Willy as he ran to the house.

"Now what happened?" asked Roman Chupp.

"Reuben told me to step over the pasture fence on stilts. He knew it had a barbed wire."

"Reuben, you didn't!" exclaimed his dad.

"No, Dad, I tried to keep him from doing tricks."

Reuben put on a confident front, but in his heart he knew that was only a half-truth.

As Reuben lay restless on his bed that night, he remembered how he had felt so hurt when Salome had fibbed about him.

He asked himself, *Why didn't I tell the whole truth?*

7
Trouble at School

A late October rain was falling steadily all night.

"This is what I call good sleeping weather," Adam remarked as they sat around the breakfast table. But for Reuben sleep had not come easily. Most of the night he lay tossing and turning, thinking of his deceptive reply to his dad the day before.

"Ya," Adam added, "I could hardly get out of bed, but I knew the chores wouldn't wait. You don't look like you were through sleeping yet either, Reuben. Guess we are all *Faulenzer* (lazybones) this morning."

Adam helped himself to the fried potatoes and passed them on to Levi, who was sitting beside him.

Reuben was glad his father hadn't asked him if he had rested well.

"I need to sack up some oats and corn to take to the mill today. If you help me, Reuben, maybe you and Salome can catch a ride to school."

"Sure, Dad." Reuben didn't feel like talking.

Salome thoroughly enjoyed riding on the back of the spring wagon atop a bag of oats covered with a tarp. She and Reuben huddled under their umbrellas and watched the raindrops march along the road behind them.

"Look, Reuben," said Salome, "it's like a bunch of people trying to catch up with us. Some of the raindrops have pretty colors. See!" she exclaimed.

Generally her chattering annoyed him, but this morning Reuben was distracted by his thoughts and only slightly acknowledged her. He was glad when they reached school.

As soon as each student was seated, Teacher John took roll call. Reuben noticed that Willy was absent. He wondered about this but was soon busy with his studies.

The rain had let up now, and by recess time the sun shone brightly. The boys headed for their ball gloves and bats, while the girls took jump ropes and ran outside. Since the ball diamond was still muddy, the boys stayed on the wet grass and practiced throwing and catching the ball.

The older girls just stood around and talked or watched the boys. Sometimes they would pass the time *Botsching*, a game similar to peas porridge hot. They would chant the words of a little ditty, clapping their hands against their partner's hands in rhythm to the rhyme.

If they missed a beat, they would laugh and giggle and start all over. The boys thought this was a silly game and suspected it was meant to attract their attention.

Today Reuben was not in a mood to do more than just return the balls thrown to him. He didn't yell or see how high he could throw the ball. But for the others, recess was a jolly time and passed too quickly. As the school bell rang calling them back to class, a lot of "ohs" and "ahs" were heard about the interruption. Nevertheless, the boys and girls broke off their play and promptly returned to the schoolhouse and their studies.

Teacher John had study plans ready: "First graders, get out your writing tablets and practice your ABCs as I have them on the chart in front of the room. Second grade, study "Henry the Bootblack," lesson 14, starting at page 35 in your *McGuffey Reader*. Third grade, do pages 31 to 33 in your spelling workbook. I will help fourth grade with fractions.

"When some of you older students have finished your work, you may help the younger ones with their lessons. But be sure your own work is done well," he warned.

Teacher John wanted his pupils to do their best. He himself had been taught as a child that whatever his hand found to do, he was to do it right.

At about eleven o'clock, the door opened and in limped Willy Chupp with two Band-Aids on the side of his face. All heads turned toward him. Reuben felt pangs of guilt when he saw him. Had Willy been hurt that badly from his fall with the stilts?

"Take your seat, Willy," directed Teacher John. "Why are you late?"

Willy just scowled.

"I asked you a question."

Reuben held his breath. Suppose Willy was late because of his accident, and it was Reuben's fault. He waited anxiously for the answer.

"My leg hurt so I could hardly walk, and my dad said he didn't have time to bring me," Willy answered.

"How did you hurt your leg?" the teacher asked—the very question Reuben feared would come up. He slumped down in his seat as if to protect himself.

"I fell" was the only information Willy offered.

What a relief to Reuben. His relief was short-lived, however. At noon recess Willy confronted him with full force.

"It's all your fault, Reuben," he yelled. "You did it. You dared me to walk those stilts across that fence, and then you said you didn't. My dad believed you and said I was lying. He gave me such a whipping with his razor strap across my legs and back. It hurts to sit or walk.

"I'm going to get you for this. I don't care if I do hurt, I'm getting even."

With those threats Willy lunged toward Reuben. Willy was much heavier than Reuben. He soon had him pinned to the ground and was pounding away.

Reuben did not want to fight. He tried to protect himself as well as he could, but Willy's fists were flying wildly.

"Run and get Teacher," Jonas Mullet called out.

Salome heard what was happening. With several others, she rushed to summon the teacher.

"Oh, *mach schnell* (hurry)!" she screamed. "*Er macht ihn dod* (he'll kill him)."

The teacher soon made an end to the ruckus and

marched both boys over to the outdoor pump to handle Reuben's bloody nose. He put a cold wet rag on the back of Reuben's neck for a few minutes and had him lean back against the front steps of the schoolhouse.

Salome and the other boys and girls had gathered around to see what would happen.

When the teacher had a chance, he told them, "You children go on with recess, and I want no fighting. Do you understand?"

The youngsters all nodded silently and went off to play in a subdued way.

Teacher John turned back to the culprits at hand. The bleeding had stopped, but they both were still breathing hard.

"What's this all about?" John asked.

Neither boy answered.

"Which of you is going to tell me?"

"I will," Willy offered.

"He made me walk stilts across a barbwire fence, then he said he didn't after I fell on the wire. My dad believed him, and he strapped me for lying. That's why my leg is hurt and why I was late. It's all his fault."

"So you thought it would make it all right by fighting it out?" asked the teacher.

Reuben could be quiet no longer. He had been miserable since telling the half-truth.

"I did wrong," he admitted. "Yes, I dared Willy to step over that fence. It's my fault he got hurt and that his dad thrashed him. I wish I wouldn't have done it. But I didn't want to fight about it."

Reuben was crying and trying to hide his tears.

"Well, I think you two boys have something to say to each other and to your parents. How about starting now?"

"I'm sorry," Reuben told Willy. "It's my fault."

Willy grunted a short sorry, but grudgingly.

"I'm expecting you to tell this to your parents," declared Teacher John.

The teacher sent them back to the pump to wash the mud and blood off their faces and hands. That helped them cool off some more. They used a wet rag to clean the worst of the mud off their clothes as well as they could. Then they ran around the schoolhouse several times to dry off.

Reuben knew his parents would find out about the fight before he had a chance to tell them. Salome would give them the whole story. Even without that, his black eye would reveal the fact that there had been trouble at school.

8
Plow a Straight Furrow

Salome couldn't run fast enough to reach home and tell what happened.

"Mom!" she shouted as she burst through the kitchen door. "Mom, *wo bist du* (where are you)?"

Lucy was coming from the pantry with a bowl of freshly churned butter. "Ach, my, *was ist letz* (what's wrong)?" she asked.

Salome was almost out of breath but tried between gasps to tell all. "Reuben was"—gasp—"Reuben, he and Willy"—gasp, sigh—"Reuben got a real"—puff, puff.

"For land's sake, Salome, stop your huffin' and puffin' and tell me," demanded Lucy, exasperated. "Here, sit down once and talk slower. Is Reuben hurt?"

"Yes, but he can walk yet. His eye is black and his jaw is swollen." Salome was finally able to offer that much information.

"*Ach, mein Zeit* (oh, my time)! What happened?"

By now Salome had calmed down considerably. She ventured to provide further details, making it as dramatic as she could.

"You should've seen it, Mom. Reuben stood his ground, but Willy hit him hard. Then Reuben said he didn't want to fight and he was sorry. He said it was all his fault."

"What was all his fault?" asked Mother.

"I don't know what Reuben meant. Willy hit him again, and Reuben fell. Then Willy held him to the ground and kept hitting him in the face, and blood was on his shirt."

"I don't want to hear any more," declared Lucy Weaver. "Where is Reuben now?"

"Oh, he's on his way home. He was walking with Abe's boys." Abe Yoders lived on the next farm west of the Weavers and were neighbors.

"Mom, Reuben's nose was bleeding *wunderbaar* (terribly). You should have seen it," Salome ventured.

"I'm glad I didn't. You go and change into your chore clothes and get the woodbox filled. Then gather the eggs."

Salome made her way to the upstairs bedroom to change. She had reveled in the importance of relating the day's happening at school, though she herself had witnessed little of what took place.

When Salome did come upon the scene, she had quickly run with others for help. However, a few eyewitnesses had told her more details. She also went by the sight of her brother, stretched what she heard, and made quite a tale.

Reuben was in no hurry to get home. He knew what

he needed to do and didn't look forward to the task. As he walked down the lane to their farm, he took his time and thought things over. Why did he let it matter when Willy called him names? His parents had told him repeatedly that Willy would have his outbursts. He knew also that many boys teased Willy.

Pushing the screen door open, Reuben encountered his mother in the kitchen.

"Mom, I suppose you know what happened at school."

"Ya, *ich duh* (I do). Salome told me. Reuben, why did you fight with Willy?"

"I didn't fight him, Mom. He hit me, but I didn't once hit him."

"You expect me to believe that?"

"Yes, Mom, I do, because it's the truth. I just tried to protect my face, but it doesn't look like I did a very good job of it." Reuben laughed lamely.

"It doesn't seem like a laughing matter to me."

"No, I guess it really isn't, and I am guilty, but not of fighting."

"What do you mean?" asked Lucy. She wasn't one to say "wait till your father gets home." She wanted the facts now.

Reuben cooperated and told her the complete truth, how he had dared Willy to step over the fence with the stilts and then shaved the truth.

"Ach, Reuben, this hurts me almost more than if you had been fighting. Go and change. We'll discuss this later tonight. I will say, though, I'm glad you confessed your wrong."

Reuben could not hide his black eye and swollen

face from the rest of the family. Levi and Jonas had seen it happening at school, but Lizzie Mae and Mandy were curious. Salome cornered them and, feeling important, began to paint as vivid a picture as she could.

"Oh, you should have seen the fight. That Willy is so *viehisch* (brutish). He almost killed Reuben. You saw how bad he looked."

Her sisters' eyes were big with wonder and fright. That is as long as her glory lasted, for her mother heard and quickly put an end to the storytelling.

Meanwhile, Reuben changed into his chore clothes and slowly made his way to the barn for milking time. He was not eager to face his father.

When Adam saw him, he exclaimed, "*Was hat gewwe mit dir* (what has happened with you)?"

"*Der Willi hat mich abgeglobbt* (Willy beat me up)," Reuben answered.

"How often have I told you not to fight?"

"Dad, I didn't fight. But it was my fault that Willy hit me."

"What did you do? I hope it wasn't name-calling."

"No, Dad. In fact, Willy called me names. Remember yesterday when Roman Chupp's came to visit and Willy got hurt walking stilts?"

"Ya, I remember," replied Adam.

"Willy called me yellow, and so I dared him to cross the pasture fence like I do."

"That fence has a barbed wire. But you said you tried to keep Willy from doing tricks!" Adam looked shocked.

"Well, at first I tried to discourage him, but then he

bragged that he could do anything better than I could. . . . He kept bugging me, so I dared him to step over the fence, and that's how he got hurt. . . ." Reuben couldn't go on talking. He was so ashamed.

"Let's get our work done, and after supper we'll settle this," Adam responded.

That meant a trip to Roman Chupps. Adam and Reuben hoped Willy's dad hadn't punished him again until he heard the whole story of what happened at school and the day before.

After the Weavers arrived, they learned that Willy's parents were not even aware of the incident at school. Roman called Willy down to the kitchen so things could be talked out.

"My son has an apology to make to you and Willy," Adam stated.

Reuben told the story just as it was and admitted to covering up part of the truth. Then he ended by saying, "I hope you won't punish Willy any more. It was my fault."

Roman Chupp scolded Willy for starting the fight, but said they wouldn't punish him any more now that they knew what happened. He thanked Adam and Reuben for coming over and settling things, and Willy gave them a wan smile.

They chatted a little while about the fall weather. Willy's mom served them each a piece of pie, and then the Weavers left.

"Son," Adam encouraged Reuben on their way home, "I'm so relieved that you told the truth."

"So am I, Dad," answered Reuben. "I feel fifty pounds lighter."

"Remember, I told you, once you can plow a straight furrow, I will buy you a horse. Well, you need to plow straight furrows in your life, too. Always be honest and upright."

Reuben went to bed with an eye and jaw that smarted, but his heart felt great. Yes, he would try from now on to plow those furrows straight. He sure would try.

9
Horseshoes and Corn Silk

Being hospitable, the Amish use every opportunity to entertain guests. Ascension Day was just such an occasion for the Weavers, and Reuben loved it. He knew it was a good time for visiting, picnics, and ball games.

Ascension Day always fell on a Thursday in the spring, forty days after Easter. It was considered a holy day, and no work was done other than caring for the animals.

Mother and Father ate no breakfast that morning, thus keeping a fast.

"May we eat?" asked Lizzie Mae. "I'm hungry. I want some mush and eggs." Fried cornmeal mush and eggs was one of her favorite breakfasts and often appeared on the table.

"Yes, you may eat," Lucy told her distraught daughter.

"Why don't you and Dad want breakfast?" Reuben inquired.

"Gather around for morning prayers, and I'll tell you," said Adam. "You all remember how Jesus died on the cross, was buried, and was raised up. Well, after forty days he went back to heaven to live with God, his Father. Here, I'll read the story to you from the end of Luke and the beginning of Acts."

After they heard the Scripture, Adam continued his explanations. "Before Jesus left, he told the disciples who saw him ascend that he would come again to receive his own. Mom and I decided to skip breakfast this morning in remembrance of his promise. We want to be ready to meet our Lord, and it is a cleansing for our body and soul to fast and pray."

"Ach, I don't need to do it then," responded Salome. "I took a good bath on Saturday."

"*Wie kindisch* (how childish)," Reuben began to mock from his vantage point of twelve years old. "You don't understand."

"Are you sure you do?" his father asked.

Reuben hung his head.

"You see," Adam continued, "we remind ourselves that we are to live in obedience to Jesus, so that when he comes back again, we will be ready."

The family prayed as Adam read from the prayer book. Then they all were left with their own thoughts.

Mother set out a light breakfast for her little brood. Since company was coming, there would be a big noon meal. She had prepared well the day before.

Two kinds of pies waited in the pie safe. A large container of chicken was ready for frying. Of course, puddings and sweets and sours were on the menu. Mashed potatoes with valleys of brown butter, gravy, stuffing, and corn rounded out the meal and, eventually, some stomachs. Coffee, too, was an absolute must.

Now, thought Reuben, *this is the good part.* His head was filled with visions of all the food and fun. Nate Wagler and his parents were coming to visit. Reuben liked Nate. Some people said he was too rowdy, but Reuben thought he was fun. There was never a dull moment with Nate in the group.

Levi Bylers were coming, also, and they had two boys, one a little older than Reuben and the other younger. There were some girls in both the visiting families, but Reuben didn't care about them.

The company arrived around ten o'clock. The girls ran for the porch swing and began lively chatter. The men found a cool and shady spot in the side yard and relaxed on lawn chairs as they visited. The women headed for the kitchen to help put the finishing touches on the noon meal and set out the food.

The boys followed Reuben to the backyard.

"Want to pitch horseshoes?" Reuben asked his guests.

The two Byler boys waited to see what Nate would say. It was plain that Nate was a leader. Reuben was not. His dad had often reassured him that it was all right to be a follower, if you are sure that your leader is doing right. Nate gave Reuben's suggestion a bit of consideration and then consented.

"I'll warn you, though," he bragged, "I'm really good at this."

Naturally, he took the first turn. Gauging the distance carefully, he threw the horseshoe toward its goal. It hooked the stake.

"A perfect ringer," Nate boasted, puffing out his chest. Time and time again, he hit his mark. At each clang of a shoe encircling the stake, Nate strutted more than ever.

"Now you try to beat that," Nate challenged Reuben, handing him a horseshoe and stepping out of range.

"That's a pretty big order to fill," Reuben responded.

His first pitch fell slightly short of its mark, but the second one hit perfectly. This gave him more confidence, and he was determined to prove his skill to Nate.

"Here come the girls," observed Joey Byler.

"That's all we need," replied Nate. "Come on, boys, let's go and hide behind the barn. I've got something to show you."

Reuben imagined Nate would perhaps show off a new pocket watch or maybe a knife. But he was in for a real surprise. Along a rail fence that guided the cows to pasture, Nate revealed his plan.

"Boys," he cautioned, "first you must promise you will not tell anyone what I'll show you. To make sure you won't, we'll all do the same. So if you tattle, you'll tell on yourself."

Reuben knew right away he shouldn't listen to Nate or go along with this escapade, but he was curious.

"Did any of you ever smoke corn silk?" Nate asked. All three boys just stood there, looking dumbfounded.

"Well, did you?" Nate repeated the question.

"No, I didn't," Reuben answered. "I don't think we should."

"Why not?" quizzed Nate. "Who will know if you don't tell? I do it all the time at home when I can sneak some of our hired man's cigarette papers. See, I've got some right here." He produced thin little white sheets. "And matches, too," he proudly announced.

"*Mir erlaawe net schpiele mit Schtreichhelzer* (we aren't allowed to play with matches)," objected Mosie Byler, the youngest of the boys.

"Who's playing? All we'll do is light them long enough to start our cigarettes. Come on, get some of this dry silk, and I'll roll them for you." Out of his pocket he pulled a plastic bag stuffed with brown corn silk.

Reuben was surprised with Nate. Even if Nate had a reputation for being rowdy, Reuben hadn't expected him to go this far. Yet since the other boys were going along with Nate's plans, Reuben also took part, against his better judgment. He didn't want them to call him a sissy.

Nate strutted and talked big, while the other boys' eyes were smarting from smoke and their throats were dry. It was a relief to Reuben and the two Byler boys when they heard the dinner bell.

"*Nau meindt, saagt nix* (now remember, don't say anything)!" Nate warned again.

The rest of the day was spoiled for Reuben because he knew he had done wrong. He had looked forward to the delicious noon meal, but when he got his food, it didn't taste as good as he had expected. He drank lots of water because his mouth was sore from the smoking experiment.

After the big meal, the boys' play was quieter in the

afternoon. Around four o'clock, the company left in time to reach home and do their evening chores.

The Weavers tended their own animals and washed up for a light supper. Reuben was quiet and thoughtful during the meal. He knew sleep would elude him unless he confessed his wrong.

"Dad," he said after supper. "Please come out on the porch for a minute. I have to talk to you."

Adam always had time to listen to his children, and he went out with his son. Reuben told him everything and felt so much better for doing so.

"Reuben, I'm glad you came and told me. I knew it already, but I'd rather that you tell me of your own free will."

"But how—how could you know?"

"Salome and the other girls followed you boys and spied on you around the corner of the barn. Then she came and told me. I guess with your sore mouth and your worries, you've suffered enough for trying to smoke."

Oh, that Molasses Face! But this time Reuben didn't care.

10
The Apple Schnitzing

The next day while they were doing chores, Adam Weaver talked some more with his son about the incident behind the barn.

"Reuben, why do you let yourself be so easily influenced by others?"

"Well, Dad, I don't want to be different, and I don't like being called a *Bobbli* (baby)."

"Would you rather do wrong, or can you stand to be different even if you are called a few names by your peers?"

"I'd rather do right, but it just seems to happen. I don't want to do bad things."

"I believe you. When temptations like these come, just remember, you will regret it if you give in."

Reuben pondered his dad's counsel, and that fall he was reminded of those wise words. It was the time of the year for cooking apple butter, and neighbors came the night before to help *schnitz* (cut) apples—bushels and bushels of them. In a year's time, a large family can use a lot of *Lattwarick* (apple butter).

Although Adam Weaver's family was not yet as large as some, they needed an ample supply of apple butter. It graced the table at every meal, to be enjoyed with homemade bread and butter. Often it was in the school lunches, too.

Many times apple butter was also used for medicinal purposes on both people and beasts. Everyone knew of its value in healing burns, and Franie Marner never came to a barn fire without it. Elam Glick even had two prize heifers that she had poulticed. Elam often said it was apple butter and Franie's quick thinking that saved those heifers. He was so *dankbaar* (thankful) for her help.

Dawdy (Grandpa) Daniel and *Mammi* (Grandma) Hildie, Adam's parents, had come to help with the *Schnitzing*. It was always fun when *Dawdies* (the grandparents) came. Tonight they brought two of the Weaver cousins along, children of Eli, Adam's brother.

Best of all, wrapped up and hidden away in the back box of Dawdies' buggy was a freezer of homemade ice cream, to enjoy after the Schnitzing was done. Reuben could hardly wait to have some.

"Dawdies are here! Dawdies are here!" squealed Salome with delight. "And they brought Erma and Sammie."

"Oh, goody," shouted Lizzie Mae. "I like to play *Lumbebopp* (rag doll) with Erma."

"Quiet down," Lucy responded firmly. "I know you're glad to see them, but such a racket might *verschrecke* (scare) them."

Reuben was equally happy to see his cousin Sammie. However, the cousins had not come just to play. Everyone with some practice in using a paring knife was soon put to work.

"Now be careful with those knives," Adam warned. "I've sharpened all of ours, and they cut deep."

Dawdy Daniel assured everyone that grandma's knives had keen edges, too.

"Oh, Mammi," said Lucy, "I'm so glad you brought your big kettles. I never have enough at Schnitzings."

"Ach, well, I brought my large dishpan, too," Hildie Weaver told her daughter-in-law.

Adam organized some outdoor projects in preparation. "Reuben, you and Sammie come to the woodshed and help me get fuel for tomorrow's cooking. I'll split the wood, and I need a few good hands to carry and stack it for me. We'll set up the copper kettle and get the stirrer down."

The copper kettle was huge. It easily held forty gallons. When not in use, it was stored in a corner of the buggy shed, and the long-handled paddle was hung on the wall above it.

Even though the kettle was covered with an old horse blanket, the whole outfit needed a good scrubbing before use. That was the women's job, and they brought pails of water and brushes to work on it.

Soon the wood was split and neatly stacked in the outer yard, a space between the barn and the well-kept, fenced lawn. The kettle sat on its three legs, with room underneath for the fire.

"I hope it won't rain tomorrow," Lucy commented. "It'll take most of the day to make apple butter."

"What will we do if it does rain?" asked Salome.

"Ach," declared Grandpa Daniel, "we'll do like they do in *Deitschland* (Germany). We'll let it rain."

Everyone laughed and found enjoyment in each other's company while working. It was a good time for jokes and fun.

"If it rains, we'll move the kettle into the buggy shed and open both end doors to let the smoke out," Adam decided.

"That's a good idea," his wife agreed.

Salome was getting tired of cutting apples. She wanted to show her cousin Erma the new gray dress her mother had recently made for her.

"I've done two bowls of apples, Mom," she said. "Can I go now?"

"Go where?" Lucy asked.

"I want to show Erma my new gray dress."

"There'll be time for that later. We work until we're finished."

Reuben was just ready to say, Ya, Molasses Face, if you weren't so slow. But he caught the words before they came out. Earlier Sammie had tempted him by suggesting they chip some of the cattle's block salt to lick. Reuben knew his dad forbade doing that, and he told Sammie about the rule.

"You're chicken," scoffed Sammy. "No one would know about it. Come on, we can wash it in the spring, and no one will find out."

Just in time, Reuben remembered his dad's words spoken that spring, and he stood his ground. He would not go along with the prank, so Sammy didn't tackle the block salt either. Instead, he looked for some other way to entertain himself.

Sammy began to taunt Salome. "Bet I can cut apples faster than you can, slowpoke."

"Ouch, oh! Look, Mom, I think I cut my hand off!" Salome screeched.

"Let me see," responded Lucy. "No, you didn't, but it is a deep cut.

"Come over here to the *Weschschissel* (wash basin). Lizzie Mae, run and get me some clean white rags. They're in the stairway closet." Lucy always saved worn-out sheets, white shirts, and even old diapers.

"Now the apple butter is really the thing we need. We'll use some to help fix your hand."

She did not put the apple butter directly on the wound. First, she washed the cut thoroughly, then cleansed it with hydrogen peroxide. After she covered the cut with a clean homemade bandage, the apple butter poultice was applied, and another clean strip of cloth covered it all.

That night when all the apples were schnitzed, the ice cream was served. Lucy had church cookies to spice up the dessert. Reuben smacked his lips in complete delight of the treat.

Salome made the most of her dilemma and played it to the hilt. You would have thought she had major surgery. She even limped when she walked. To anyone who would listen, she kept repeating, "Oh, my hand hurts."

"Maybe you'd better lie down awhile," Adam told his daughter. "I don't suppose you want any ice cream."

"Ach, I think ice cream would make me feel better!"

67

Reuben did feel sorry for Salome because it had happened after Sammie made fun of her. He wondered if Sammie felt inner turmoil as he did whenever he caused problems.

"Hey, Sis," he told Salome, "tomorrow I will give you a penny to throw into the apple butter, and it will come out all shiny and bright, like new."

That made her feel better. Her brother cared.

"*Danki* (thanks)," she said.

"You're welcome, *Melaasich Gsicht.*"

Salome grinned a big happy grin. She felt fine.

11
Deitsch Is Best

"Reuben," said Adam Weaver one morning, "I want you to go to town with mother today. I'm going to the horse sale, so I can't take her.

"Mol has thrown a shoe, so you'll need to use Star. Now that you're thirteen, I think you can handle her with Mom along to keep you from driving too fast!" He gave Reuben a grin.

Even though Reuben was thrilled and felt grown-up at the confidence his father placed in him, he also was a bit disappointed.

"But Dad, I thought maybe I could go along to the sale," Reuben protested. His longing and hope of finding his dream horse had never left him.

"Not this time. Perhaps next month we can work it out."

But next month the summer vacation would be over, and Reuben would be back in the classroom. The horse auctions always took place on Fridays, and he knew his dad wouldn't let him miss school to go along. Well, he decided, there was nothing to do except wait and hope.

Lucy Weaver sent Lizzie Mae across the field to the neighbor's. She was to ask if one of the older Yoder girls could come and stay with the children until she returned from town.

"Mom," offered Salome, "I could take care of the other children until you and Reuben get back. I'm old enough."

"Not just yet," her mother stated. "For an eleven-year-old, you're a big help around the house, but I'll feel better if one of the neighbor girls is here. Anyhow, it'll be fun for you to have someone else around."

It wasn't long until Lizzie Mae returned with Nancy Yoder.

"I'm glad you could come, Nancy," Lucy welcomed her. "I hope your mother could spare you."

"Ach, ya. With four girls around the house, we can always spare one."

"It shouldn't take long to do my errands in town. Reuben is driving me there, and Adam is away at a horse sale."

"No need to hurry on my account. Is there anything you would like me to do while you're gone?"

"You need only watch the children. I've given them a few jobs to keep them out of trouble."

"I see Salome is picking lima beans. She could probably use some help there."

"Suit yourself, then. Reuben will be going with me. Lizzie Mae will help with the bean picking and shelling. Levi and Jonas are sweeping cobwebs in the barn,

70

and Mandy will be taking a nap. I hope they're not too much bother."

"They won't be," Nancy assured Lucy.

"Nancy, maybe you could take this box with cartons of eggs out to the buggy, and I'll carry the kettle of butter."

"I'll be glad to help, Lucy."

By then Reuben was waiting by the front yard gate with the rig. "Come, Mom, Star is anxious to go. See how she prances!"

"Ach my," remarked his mother. "I hope you can handle her good."

"Don't worry. I can. She just wants to run."

When they turned from the farm lane into the roadway, Star broke into a trot.

"*Heb sie ein* (hold her back)," Lucy advised her son.

Reuben was thoroughly enjoying himself. He did keep a tight rein on Star to please his mother and put her fears at ease. How he would love to give Star a free rein! Reuben wondered exactly how fast she could go.

His thoughts ran free. Willy Chupp and his cousin, Sammie, would sure be jealous if they could see him driving by. At least he could impress them next Sunday when he would tell them about the trip.

It took only about half as long to travel the distance with Star as it took with Mol. As they entered town, Reuben slowed Star to a walk.

"Be sure you tie Star *gut* (securely)," Lucy told Reuben as they pulled up to the hitching pole.

"Ya, Mom," Reuben answered. "I will."

Star's sides were glistening with sweat, and Reuben patted her gently as he walked back to help his mother.

"Bring the box of eggs, and I'll get the kettle of butter," Lucy told her son.

Several of the local merchants were regular customers for the butter and eggs. Her products sold well and were always of best quality.

After disposing of her wares, Lucy told Reuben to take the empty basket and kettle back to the buggy and check Star. "Make sure Star is alright, and then meet me at the mercantile."

The mercantile or general store carried anything from groceries to chicken wire. Lucy would look over what they had on sale and then use the butter-and-egg money to purchase a few things.

The pavement seemed hot as Reuben went back to the buggy. He found Star firmly tied, flicking flies, and nickering to the other horses at the hitching post. After he petted Star a little, he pulled an apple out of his pocket, put it on his palm, and offered it to the horse. Star chomped it down with gusto.

Reuben didn't mean to linger, but he spent more time than he realized in talking to Star and checking the other horses. In his estimation, Star was in a class by herself. Only the horse he planned to own one day would surpass her.

When Reuben finally returned to the mercantile, he found his mother the object of some attention she didn't want. The new clerk and even several young *englisch* boys were laughing at her.

"What else did you say you wanted, Mrs. Weaver?"

"A jug of win-e-gar," Lucy pronounced it plainly this time.

"Well now, let's see, we have vinegar, if that's what

you want," said the clerk. "Yes, sir, we have good White Mule Vinegar."

"That's what I want, then," Lucy answered, embarrassed.

"Win-e-gar, huh!" He imitated her and laughed outright as did the boys who were poking fun at her speech.

"Vil der be some-sing else?" he asked, mocking Lucy's Amish accent.

"No," Lucy answered.

The clerk bagged the purchases and opened the cash register. "Den dats sirteen dollars and sirty sree cents."

Lucy paid her bill and left with her son carrying the jug of vinegar and a bag of cooking supplies. They packed the things securely in the back buggy box, and Reuben untied Star and headed out of town. Star was always eager to go home, and they moved along at a brisk clip.

"Oh, Mom, why do people have to make fun of us?" Reuben asked.

"Ach, they don't have to, Reuben. They just don't know any better," Lucy told her son.

"Well, I don't like them making *Schpott* (fun) of you."

"Don't let it trouble you, Reuben. *Es geht mit ihnen heem* (it will go home with them). They'll have to deal with it."

"Are you going back to that store again?" Reuben asked.

"We don't have much of a choice, do we? It's the only mercantile in town. Mr. Jackson owns the store, and he knows we bring good business his way. He respects us. If he ever hears such disrespect for customers some day, he'll straighten out that clerk in a hurry."

Star also was in a hurry, but Reuben managed her well. He, too, was anxious to be home, for he planned to tell his dad how his mother was mistreated.

Lucy hadn't planned on saying a word to Adam. After all, she knew, the Amish expected to be ridiculed for their beliefs and their plain way of life.

"Dad," declared Reuben, "I wouldn't go back to Jackson Mercantile."

"Ach, Reuben, we can't let such things hurt us. It keeps us humble."

"I still don't like to hear my mom being laughed at. It isn't fair."

"Reuben, the next time I need *Essich* (vinegar), I'll ask for a jug of White Mule. The clerk will know what I mean. If everyone would just speak our way, then it wouldn't be so different."

"*Deitsch* (German) is best," said Lucy.

"Yes, *Deitsch* is best and comes easier."

Reuben agreed.

12
Our Maust Book

"Lizzie Mae, run out and see if the mail has come."

It was after lunch, and Lucy Weaver liked to look at the mail before she took a short afternoon rest.

This was *Budget* day at the Weaver's—a day of anticipation. *The Budget* was a weekly newspaper compiled mostly for and by the Amish. One might say it was made up of letters from home folks near and far.

The pages of *The Budget* would reveal who had a new baby and whether it was a dishwasher (girl) or woodchopper (boy). It regularly reported who ate Sunday dinner with whom, where church services were to be held, and what weather and crop conditions were at the writer's place.

"Here's the mail, Mom," said Lizzie Mae, handing her mother a large bundle.

"You children go and play quietly now while I read *The Budget*," Lucy directed. She was totally ignoring the letters and farm papers.

Time passed so quickly when she was reading the news. Lucy found out that Gideon Zooks had another woodchopper. This outnumbered their dishwashers by three. The family consisted of six girls and nine boys! *My,* thought Lucy, *Effie Zook sure must have her hands full.*

Leffy Noah's Sam wrote about one of their cows having twins, but not on the same day. One was born five minutes before midnight, and the other one eight minutes after.

Then, of course, there were the obituaries. Lucy also read the shower announcements and, whenever possible, would send a card to cheer someone or a little money to help with expenses. She knew what it meant to be part of a sharing, caring people.

Often a friend or relative sent a short request to *The Budget* about a lonely shut-in needing encouragement, or a family suffering from hospital expenses or loss of buildings by fire. Many sufferers took heart again from this simple act of love in passing on word of need and in the responses from readers such as Lucy.

"Mom," said Salome, "I found this letter by the front porch steps. Lizzie Mae must have dropped it. You should let me get the mail. Lizzie Mae is *schusslich* (careless)."

"I am not," Lizzie Mae objected.

"Oh, it could happen to anyone," Lucy reminded her daughters.

"Let's see the letter. Ach, my! It's from Rebecca and James. We haven't heard from them for a while. Wonder what could have happened."

"Why don't you open it?" asked Salome. "Maybe

nothing happened. Perhaps she wants us to come and visit."

The girls watched as their mother began reading.

"Well my land, I can't believe it! Ach, no! Oh, I don't think we could."

"What, Mom, what did Rebecca say?"

"Oh, *mein Zeit* (my time), why did they pick us?"

"Pick us for what? Tell us," said Salome.

"The *Freindschaft* (relatives) want someone to get a Maust book together, and Rebecca says we were chosen."

Lucy put the letter aside. "We'll have to see what Dad says, but now we must get back to work."

During supper that evening, Lucy gave Adam the letter to read, and they began discussing the book proposal.

"What's a Maust book?" Reuben asked.

"It's a report of our family tree," Adam told him. "Our people are interested in who our forebears are and where they came from. We like to see how far back our roots go and collect stories about the lives of those who have gone before us."

"I know my great-great-grandparents traced their ancestors to Bern, Switzerland," Lucy volunteered.

"Switzerland! I wonder, could they yodel then?" Levi asked.

"Ach, what difference does it make?" Reuben remarked. If a book wasn't about horses, he didn't think it was worth reading.

"Well, I heard that all Swiss people are good yodelers, and now that I know we come from there, I'm going to try it too," Levi declared.

"Oh, *schon uns, sei so gut* (spare us, please)!" Reuben exclaimed.

"Now, boys, let's not argue," their dad intervened. "I don't think the Amish had much to do with yodeling, although it might have been handy in calling back and forth to each other in the mountains. Our ancestors left Europe because of persecution, war, and hard times. We've found a safe place to live here, even if people do make fun of us once in a while. At least we can have our own farms."

"What shall we do about this Maust book proposal?" asked Lucy.

"Well, dear wife, if you're willing to write most of the letters, let's see what we can gather for a Maust book. A lot of interesting stories will come to us, and we can put them together in order. We'll likely have to sketch out a family tree to keep it all straight. I'm sure our relatives will be excited to read about themselves and their ancestors when we get the book out."

"Ya, then, let's do it," replied Lucy eagerly.

Levi, however, was stuck on his Swiss background. For several weeks Reuben endured the caterwauling sounds of Levi's attempts at yodeling. His practice was out of earshot of the rest of the family, as the boys were busy at chores or doing various tasks on the farm. Reuben snorted at Levi's weird sound production, but he was not one to tattle.

Then one evening Adam heard Levi perform and solved the problem with dispatch.

"Levi, from now on you yodel only when you're out in the woods or somewhere alone."

Reuben was relieved and overjoyed.

The next months were filled with much letter writing and research. Being Amish and thus without telephones, Lucy and Adam obtained information for the Maust book through correspondence and visits with various relatives.

Reuben found it fun to read all the letters from many different states telling of happenings years before he was born. He kept his ears open, listening for any important information.

This book would not only contain the lineage of each family, but some events during different generations. Reuben learned that in pioneer times one of their ancestors purchased some land from a Shawnee Indian tribe. Only a few white families were living in that area then. Once in a while, the Indians would drop in for a meal with their Amish neighbors.

One evening Reuben heard his parents talk of an *englisch* man who came from the canton of Bern, Switzerland. He and his family were poor. Finally he found work as a teamster on a towpath beside a canal along the Delaware River. During the Revolutionary War, the husband was seized by a group of soldiers.

At the close of the war, he came home to find that his wife had passed away. While dying, she was greatly concerned about what would happen to her five small children. She was impressed by the quiet, peace-loving Amish Mennonite people and requested that her children be reared in their homes.

"Well then," mused Lizzie Mae, "maybe we are part *englisch*."

"Does that make us worldly?" Salome asked.

"Ach *du leiber, nee* (my land, no)!" exclaimed Lucy.

"A person's ancestors don't make us worldly. It's what's in the heart and what we ourselves do."

"We need to find someone to print the book, once we have all the information together," planned Adam. "I hear there's a man in Wayne County who has a little printshop in the basement of his home. We'll go and see him once we're ready."

"Some people are so slow in answering my letters and supplying the information I need. I hate to keep writing and asking again. How long does it take to write the names of your parents and grandparents, plus those of your children and their spouses and children?" Lucy asked, exasperated.

"I know," Adam answered. "It's a big job. I hope we can get it done accurately."

On Friday there was a large amount of mail. After supper the family sat at the kitchen table and shared each letter.

Reuben was surprised when his father read a letter from Oregon. One named Simeon Weaver had been a stableboy and groomsman for the Archbishop of Canterbury.

This naturally set Reuben to speculating about what all his ancestors were involved in. He sure wished his parents would hurry and finish this book. Never did he think he would care for something in print unless "his" horse were in it, but the Maust book would be special.

13
Willy Spends the Night

Adam Weaver was ready to retire for the night when he heard someone on his front porch. He made his way to the kitchen and met Roman Chupp opening the door and stepping inside.

"Well, Roman, come on in," Adam greeted him, although Roman was already inside. "I couldn't imagine who was coming."

"Ya, it's late," said Roman. "I have a death message."

"Oh." This always struck a certain fear into Adam's heart. Who could it be this time?

"Erkel had a call from Indiana saying old Jonas Raber passed away."

Joe Erkel was an *englisch* friend who picked up vegetables to take to market. He was designated for the local South district of the Amish to receive and deliver important phone messages. Once in a while a list was printed in *The Budget* informing people all over North America whom to contact in the various areas if they needed to get urgent word to relatives and friends.

"The missus and I plan to go, and we were asked to let you know. Do you think you'll attend?" Roman asked.

"Oh, I'm sure we will, or at least I want to go. Could you wait a bit while I talk to Lucy?"

"Sure," agreed Roman, "take your time."

"Make yourself comfortable. I should be back in a minute."

Roman sat down in the old hickory rocker. He spied the *Farmer's Guide* magazine and began to page through it. Adam made his way to the bedroom, but his wife was not there.

"Lucy's the workingest woman I've ever known," he told Roman as he walked back into the kitchen.

"I thought she'd gone to bed after our *Owed Gebet* (evening prayer), but she must have remembered an unfinished job. She's probably weeding a *Blummeland* (flowerbed) or working in the garden. As long as there's a bit of daylight left, she makes use of it."

He laughed as he headed for the back door. "I won't be long."

"Take your time," Roman responded. "I've found an interesting article here to read." Besides, something else was preying on Roman's mind.

Just as Adam suspected, he found his wife busily weeding a flower bed. "I thought you'd gone to bed already. Now I find you out here hunting for weeds," he teased.

"There's no need to hunt. They're here alright. You can help me if you like, and then I'll be in sooner."

"I would," answered Adam, "only I can't. Roman

Chupp is here waiting for an answer from me."

"Well, I didn't hear anyone come."

"Of course not. You're at the far side of the house, away from the drive."

"Well, what does he want?" asked Lucy.

"He came with a message. Jonas Raber from Indiana passed away. Romans are hiring a van to take them and thought we might want to go."

"Ach, my, I'd like to, but I don't see how I can get away. I have two batches of pickles going. I must change the salt solution every day for three days yet so they'll be ready to can. And anyhow, someone has to look after the children."

"Why don't we go in and talk with Roman and make our decision?" Adam suggested.

After further discussion, they decided that Adam would go but Lucy would stay and tend to things at home. Adam would have preferred to have her accompany him, but he understood.

"Now," Roman commented, clearing his throat, "I have a problem. We don't think it wise to have Willy go with us. He gets excited in a large group of people and it makes *die Fraa* (the wife) very nervous.

"I know it would mean trouble to leave him at home with the hired man. Would it be too much to ask to have him stay at your place, Lucy, for one night? He and Reuben are together a lot, and I think he might behave better for you."

Lucy had some misgivings and hardly knew what to say. Still, the Christian and neighborly thing was to say yes. So it happened that Friday morning found Willy at the Weaver home.

"Now, *sei en guter Bu* (be a good boy) and mind Lucy," Willy's mother instructed. She was dubious about the outcome of his stay with Lucy and her family.

"Ach, don't worry," Lucy tried to assure her. But she herself was not very confident.

Adam gave Reuben instructions about seeing that the chores were done morning and evening. He listed some tasks around the buildings that Reuben and Levi were to do while he was gone.

"Now, Reuben," Adam declared in parting, "you're fourteen, and here's your chance to show what a man you are. I'm trusting you to keep things going well while I'm away. Willy can work along with you and Levi. If you act sensibly, you'll be a good example for the younger ones. And do what your mother says. When I get back, I'll want to hear how it went."

Then Adam was off in the van with Roman Chupps and a few others going to Indiana. Reuben watched the line of dust trailing the van out the lane and down the gravel road. This would be a big event as Amish people gathered from far and near. They would renew friendships while saying good-bye to old Jonas and committing him to the Lord.

Meanwhile, Reuben was in charge of the farm work. "I have to clean out the horse barn today," Reuben told Willy. "You can help. If two of us work together, we'll get done sooner, and then maybe we can do other things."

"Like what?" Willy wanted to know.

"You choose. What would you like to do?" Reuben asked.

"Why don't we rob birds' nests and cross the baby birds' wings so they won't be able to fly. Or fish for minnows in the pond and cut them in two so we can watch them wiggle."

"Ach, Willy," Reuben objected, "how mean can you be! Those creatures have feelings. We're big enough to know better than to do stuff like that."

"All right, then, I won't help you work"

Several times Reuben was interrupted in his chores because of Willy. If Willy wasn't tormenting the cats, he was chasing the baby calf or letting the sheep out of their pens.

The real problem took place at bedtime. After a good meal of cold milk and banana soup, half-moon pies, and late garden lettuce, the older children went outdoors. They played tag and then, as dusk dropped over the yard and fireflies lit the air, they had fun with the game of no bears out tonight.

"*Kummt—Bettzeit* (come—bedtime)," Lucy called. Everyone responded willingly, except Willy. However, when he saw no one stayed to play, he reluctantly followed. After washing their dirty feet in a large tin tub, the older children made their way upstairs.

Reuben was tired and ready to go to sleep. Not Willy. He was in bed and then instantly out again.

Willy removed the chimney from the kerosene lamp and was holding a comb in the flames.

"What are you doing?" asked Reuben.

"I want to see if it'll burn."

"No, don't!" Reuben jumped out of bed and tried to wrestle the comb from Willy. In the scuffle the lamp tipped over and the dresser scarf caught fire.

85

"See what you made me do!" Willy accused Reuben.

Reuben was quick in thought and action. He grabbed his pillow and smothered the flame.

Lucy heard the noise and also smelled the smoke. She got the full story from her son as she entered his upstairs room. Of course, Willy tried to pin the blame on Reuben.

"I think it's best if I make a *Boddenescht* (floor nest, bed) in the living room for Willy."

Neither she nor Reuben slept well until after three in the morning, when Willy finally settled down.

Lucy wondered how Willy's mother could cope, but she told herself, *God must give her special strength.*

As for Reuben, he would not soon forget when Willy spent the night.

Late the next evening the vanload returned from Indiana, and Willy's parents took him home. Adam talked about all the people with whom he had visited, and Lucy and Reuben told him about Willy's pranks. They all wondered what would become of Willy if he kept on being so unruly.

"Let's remember to pray for Roman Chupps and especially for Willy," suggested Adam. "They need our encouragement."

14
Mystery in the Oat Bin

Reuben knew right off that it wasn't right. But Willy always had such interesting things to show him. This Sunday, church was held at Adam Weavers' home again, and after the noon meal, Willy Chupp enticed Reuben to go aside with him—alone.

"*Was wit* (what do you want)?" asked Reuben.

"I've got something to show you. I found it in the hired hand's room."

"Did you steal it?" asked Reuben. "You know stealing is wrong."

"No, I didn't steal it. I just borrowed it for a little bit. I'll give it back."

"Well, it's stealing, if you don't ask."

"Do you want to see what it is, or don't you?"

"I guess I shouldn't," Reuben answered.

"Aw, come on. You'll really like it. I hid it in our buggy under the lap robe."

Against his better judgment, Reuben followed. Willy looked this way and that and then quickly removed an article from the buggy and slipped it under his shirt. He started walking past the outbuildings and motioned to Reuben to follow.

"Come on, let's go behind the barn so no one will see us."

Reuben already felt wicked. If they had to hide, then he knew it was wrong.

"What is it, Willy? What do you have?"

"Here," said Willy, thrusting a magazine into Reuben's hand. "Look at that animal. Isn't it something?"

Reuben's eyes opened wide as he saw on the cover a picture of the horse of his dreams.

"Wow!" he exclaimed.

"Now look inside. There's a whole story about him and the races he won. And girls, too," laughed Willy.

"He is one beautiful horse, Willy, but no, I can't read it. There isn't time now and. . . ."

Reuben didn't get to finish his sentence before Willy offered, "Just keep it and hide it, then give it back later."

"No, Willy," decided Reuben. "As much as I'd like to read all about that horse, I can't do that."

"Well, why not? I hide things all the time. Anyway, if I'm found out, I can make up a good story or get real upset and cry so they'll pity me."

Reuben thought how awful that would be. He did pity Willy, but for a different reason.

"We'd better go now," Reuben insisted again as he turned his back and walked off.

"*Du bist dumm* (you're dumb)," Willy told him.

That remark bothered Reuben a bit as he made his way back to the other boys. But he was able to put it behind him when he remembered what his father had told him one time: "Things only upset you as much as you let them."

Later in the afternoon, most of the people had gone to their homes. Adam was removing benches from various rooms of their house and stacking them in the church wagon. These benches were used to sit on during the three-and-a-half-hour service. They were carted from place to place in a closed-in *Bankwagge* (bench wagon).

"Here, Reuben," requested Adam, "give me a hand."

Reuben grabbed the other end of a bench and helped carry it to the wagon. Then they went back for more.

Lucy had invited a few close friends and relatives for the evening meal. It would be a simple fare of lunchmeat sandwiches, potato salad, fruit, cake, and coffee, tea, or lemonade.

"Are we having a singing tonight?" Reuben asked.

"Yes, Mom thought we should. She said we need to do what we can to keep our *Yunge* (young folks) in the church, and I agree with her," Adam replied.

Reuben was glad there would be a singing at his place. He would have a chance to see how it was done. In another year he would be sixteen and on *Rumschpringe* (running around with the young folks). How exciting that would be!

Then he began to visualize it: Yes, he was driving to singing with his special horse, and none of the other

Buwe (boys) could keep up with Prince.

"What, daydreaming again?" Adam broke in to his thoughts. "I've been standing here holding my end of the bench. Grab your end, and maybe we'll get finished clearing these rooms by chore time."

Reuben came back to reality with a start. He must pay attention and do his part. Perhaps they would let him stay up until singing was over. He knew if he had to go to bed with the younger ones, he couldn't sleep anyway.

Salome would beg to stay up later, too. He was sure of that. Sometimes he had to do things for Salome's sake.

It was almost chore time, and Reuben was anxious to get the task done. He rushed with his end of the next bench.

"Now why are you in such a hurry?" Adam asked his son.

"I want to be done with chores before time for the singing."

"You will be, the way you've been jumping around," Adam assured him. "Now let's leave these last benches in the kitchen for the *Yunge* when they come for singing."

The farm kitchen was large and provided the best gathering place, with lead singers around the table and benches for others.

Adam closed up the church wagon temporarily and headed for the barn to start chores. Reuben was on the porch and about to follow. Just then, through the screen door he overheard a conversation in the kitchen.

"May I stay up for the singing?" Salome asked her mother.

Reuben just knew this would happen. He waited for the answer.

"Well, you're almost fourteen. Let's see what your father thinks."

Reuben was in suspense until his dad decided. Right after they came to the house after chores, the parents huddled to discuss the matter. Then the answer came through Lucy.

"Salome, you may stay and listen to the singing, but you'll sit with us in the living room."

"What about Reuben?" Salome asked.

"Dad and I agreed that he may sit just outside the *Schtuppdaer* (room door) so he can see the *Yunge*—if he behaves."

That made Reuben feel very grown-up. Salome wanted to be at the door with Reuben, but she did not complain, however, for fear of losing the privilege granted her.

"Where are you going?" Lucy asked her husband after supper.

"Ach, I forgot to give Star some extra oats. She has been a bit off her feed, and I want to put some of that medicine in the oats for her. That's the only way I can get her to take it."

"I hope you won't be long. The *Yunge* (young folks) will come soon."

"Ya, I won't be long," Adam replied.

He made his way to the granary and the oat bin. As he proceeded to scoop up a bit of oats, something caught his eye in the dim light. Adam drew back his hand and waited. Whatever he saw didn't move.

Taking the scoop, he pushed the grain around, and there it was: a magazine with a picture of a horse on the cover. Adam paged through the articles and then checked the address label. It was mailed to Roman Chupp's hired hand. But how in the world did it find its way into their oat bin?

As he pondered this, he wondered if Reuben had anything to do with it. He knew Reuben's love for horses. Surely, though, they had taught their son well enough and instilled the fear of Almighty God in him so that he would not sneak around with someone else's magazine, and such a worldly one, at that.

Well, he must take care of Star now, and he would not spoil the evening's singing by bringing this up. Tomorrow would be time enough to confront Reuben and try to solve this mystery of the oat bin. *Sufficient unto the day is the evil thereof,* Adam reflected.

15

Thanks, Molasses Face

Reuben was thoroughly enjoying the evening. Many young folks had gathered for the singing. He watched as the girls and the best singers filed in and sat down around the large oblong oak kitchen table, lit by two large lamps. Others found room on benches placed around the room. Everyone seemed to be in such a happy mood.

There were a few stragglers outside, and Adam encouraged them to join the gathering inside. "You're welcome to come in," Adam told them. "We opened our home to you and would like to have you sing with the rest of the group. So just come on."

"Well, maybe if we get a notion and don't find anything *besser* (better) to do," smirked Lefty Joe. He was a show-off, and it didn't help matters for Adam when the other boys broke out with boisterous laughter.

"Just remember, my door is always open," Adam declared, turning back to the porch.

Reuben heard the conversation and respected his father's wise attitude. He did not show anger nor did he try arguing to force the boys to come in.

The girls at the singing looked neat with their plain-colored dresses, white aprons, capes, and head coverings.

Reuben wondered why the girls wore black coverings to preaching on Sunday morning, but in the evening wore white coverings. He thought perhaps it was so the boys could see how they would look after they became a *Fraa* (wife) and put on a white covering all the time. He would ask Salome.

Levi and Salome begged to sit out by the kitchen door with Reuben for a better view of the *Yunge*.

"Ach," said Lucy, "soon enough you join them. Tonight you stay by my chair and listen."

Salome pouted. Reuben was only a year and a half older than she was. It did not seem fair, but she obeyed nonetheless.

"Turn to page one in the little book," announced Thrasher Jake's Mose.

He needn't have announced the page number because this song was *always* sung first. It was the beautiful "Loblied," a German praise song to God.

The singing was different from that at morning services. They did not sing with the slow *Weis* (tune), but at a moderate pace with four-part harmony. The melody was so nice that even Jonas, Mandy, and Lizzie Mae listened.

For about a half hour the German hymnbook was used. Then they paused to refresh their voices with cool drinks of water from the pitchers and glasses placed on the table for their convenience.

The younger children were sent off to bed during this break, but Reuben and Salome were allowed to stay up. After the singing started again, it changed to include English hymns.

Now for the first time, Reuben heard these English songs, and he loved them also. One refrain especially impressed him: "On Christ the solid rock I stand, all other ground is sinking sand." He knew he would remember that song. Maybe it would help steady him when friends like Willy tempted him with wild schemes.

Just then there was a loud bang right outside the kitchen window. Girls screamed, and all singing stopped.

"Ach my, *was is letz* (what's the matter)?" gasped Lucy, reaching out to hold Salome close in the confusion.

"I don't know, but I aim to find out," her husband replied.

"Be careful," Lucy cautioned.

A small group of boys were standing by the cistern and laughing.

"What's going on out here?" Adam asked.

Lefty Joe spoke up in his cocky manner. "We have a few firecrackers left from last Fourth of July and just wanted to add a little spark to the goody bunch in there. Get it—firecracker—spark?"

The boys outside howled with laughter. It was plain to see that they weren't sober. In fact, Melvin Plank had a bottle in his hand.

"Boys, I feel sorry for you, and I must ask you to

leave. This gathering is to praise the Lord. If you can't join in that, then go on home."

"Oh, so now he is throwing us off his place. Well, boys, what do you say. Shall we throw him over the fence?"

"I wouldn't do that if I were you," Adam told them.

"*Fer was net* (why not)?" bellowed Lefty Joe. "You think we can't?"

"Sure you can," responded Adam calmly, "but I wouldn't advise it unless you want to explain it to your parents."

That did it. One by one the young whipper-snappers got their rigs and left.

The rest of the evening passed peacefully. Adam expressed his appreciation to the faithful young folks who sang praises to God.

On Monday morning the family went about their usual work. After chores and breakfast, Adam and Reuben loaded the rest of the benches onto the church wagon and closed it up. It was ready to be pulled to the home where services would be held in two weeks.

"Reuben, I'll take you to school," Adam informed his son. "There's something we need to talk about."

Reuben could not imagine what it would be, but he was glad for the opportunity to ride to school.

"May we come along, too?" asked Salome for herself and the younger children.

"Not this time," said Adam, and he looked very somber.

"I need to talk to Reuben alone."

What could it be? Reuben wondered. He couldn't think of any wrongdoing that might be blamed on him.

When they turned from the drive and onto the road, Adam produced from under his jacket the very magazine Willy had shown Reuben that Sunday after church.

"What do you know about this?" Adam asked.

"Dad, why Dad, that looks exactly like a magazine Willy Chupp showed me!" Reuben exclaimed. He was dumbfounded.

"Showed it to you, huh? Then what was it doing in our oat bin?"

"What! Dad, I don't know."

"Reuben, are you telling me the truth?"

"Yes, Dad, I am."

"Then explain how it got in my bin. Where does Willy get these things?"

"I can't explain how it got where it did, but Willy said he took it from their hired man's room."

"Well, Reuben, you have all day to think about this. Tonight I want a straight answer."

All day Salome could tell that something was troubling Reuben. Although he teased her, she did not like to see him sad. When school was over and they were on the way home, she dropped back from the group of girls and signaled Reuben to pull away from the boys walking in a clump.

"I'll walk home with you," Salome offered. "What's wrong, Reuben? You didn't play ball today. Tell me what's bothering you."

Reuben was surprised at her question, and then he found himself confiding in his sister. He told about the magazine Willy showed him and how later his dad found it in the oat bin. "And that's the whole story," he concluded. "I didn't do it, but Dad thinks I did."

"Ach my, Reuben, I know how that magazine got in the bin. I and Wally's Maudie sneaked out and watched what Willy showed you. We heard what you said, that you didn't want to keep it. Well, after you left, Willy went into the granary. Then he came out without the book. I was going to look for it later, but didn't get a chance."

"Oh, thanks, Molasses Face. Now I can tell Dad. I didn't know what to do. Thanks. I'm glad you're my sister, and this time I'm glad you snooped!"

16
It's Ready

Adam called his family to gather in the living room after supper. "We have a problem that needs to be taken care of," he stated. "I think it's good if you all hear what I have to say."

Reuben knew what he was going to talk about but decided not to interfere.

"Last night," Adam continued, "I found this magazine hidden in the oat bin. Reuben said he didn't put it there. I talked to him about it on the way to school this morning. I hope he's telling the truth, but someone must have done it. Do any of you know how it came to be hidden there?"

There was absolute silence.

"Levi?" Adam directed his attention to his second son. Levi was as bewildered as his dad was and only shook his head.

"What about you, Salome? I would hope not, but did you hide it?"

Reuben felt sure Salome would tell all, but she only shook her head.

It was time to speak up, so Reuben began: "Dad, I want to tell you something."

"Oh, then it was you, Reuben. Why couldn't you own up to it this morning? I struggled with this matter all day.

"Children, I hope you will take a lesson from this. You cannot do wrong and get away with it. Sooner or later, it will come out. You will need to be punished, and I suppose the hardest thing for you would be to miss the horse sale I was going to take you to, Reuben."

Mother sat in her rocker, tears streaming down her cheeks. How could their firstborn son be so *hinne rum* (behind their backs)?

"But wait, Dad," burst out Salome. "Reuben didn't do it."

"*Was nau* (what now)?" asked Adam in amazement. "Salome, do you mean to tell me you did it? You hid that magazine?"

"No, Dad, she didn't," Reuben assured him, "but we know who did."

"We?" asked Adam.

"Yes, Salome and I know."

"Well, *raus mit* (out with it)!"

"Willy Chupp hid that magazine."

"But when? How?"

"When church was here yesterday, Willy asked me to go out to their buggy so he could show me something. I went, and then he wanted me to follow him behind the barn. There he tried to get me to take the magazine and read it. He wanted me to give it back later at school."

"Ei-yi-yi-yi," moaned Lucy. "Why did you do it, Reuben?"

"But Mom, I didn't. I refused to take the magazine. Salome and Wally's Maudie followed us. Salome said that after I went back to the other boys, she saw Willy go in our granary with that magazine, and when he came out, he didn't have it."

"Why didn't you tell us about it, Salome?" Adam asked his daughter.

"I was afraid Willy would get mad at me if I told."

"Tomorrow I'll go by the Chupp place and give this back," declared Adam. "We've all learned a lesson tonight. You children can see that it doesn't pay to do what is wrong, and I learned not to blame others until I know all the facts. Reuben, I'm sorry I blamed you. Will you forgive me?"

Reuben was touched by his father's humility. What should he say?

"Ya," he answered, his voice quavering.

"Well, I guess we will all sleep better tonight. Now let's have our *Owed Gebet* (evening prayer), and then we'd better get to bed. Mom looks tired, and I know I am."

Reuben lay a long time looking out his bedroom window at the many twinkling stars. He thought how kind his parents were and that maybe his sister Salome wasn't half bad after all. Perhaps he was learning to stand on "the solid rock" and not be swayed when Willy proposed something out of line.

On Saturday the Weavers were back at their usual

weekend tasks. Mother and the girls cleaned and baked in preparation for Sunday. The house must be spotless. Later, there would be girls' hair to wash and braid, and boys' hair to cut.

After lunch, though, Lucy Weaver decided to take a short nap. Each afternoon she gave herself this luxury. Today she was awakened by the shouts of Jonas and Lizzie Mae.

"Look, Mom," they exclaimed, "we brought the mail in for you, and here is a package!"

"Whatever can it be? I didn't send to the mail order for anything."

Mother examined the package carefully. The return label had a Wayne County address. Yes, of course, now it dawned on her.

"Why, these must be our first copies of the *Maust Family History.*"

Lucy hurriedly opened the box. Sure enough, there they were, six free samples, just as they had been promised.

"Would you look at that, children?" Lucy rejoiced, her eyes sparkling. "Isn't the cover a pretty blue?"

She wished she could sit right down and look at each page. That would just have to wait until tomorrow. *Sunday afternoon will be a good time for that,* she thought. She placed the books on top of her bureau, out of the reach of little hands.

"Come, children, we must get back to work."

Lucy baked five pies and a cake, scrubbed little heads clean, washed windows, fixed potato salad for Sunday, cleaned and polished both the kitchen and heating stoves, all before chore time. She would braid her little girls' hair just before they retired. This gave their long tresses more time to dry.

Reuben had been plowing for winter wheat. He was almost sixteen now, and this would be his last year in school. The law said you had to go until you were sixteen. Reuben didn't understand why. He thought he was learning enough from his parents on the farm to make a go of it in life.

Instead of being in school, he would much rather be walking or riding along behind a team of good strong workhorses, watching the rich black soil turn up as he worked. He wondered if those who made the laws could plow a straight furrow. He knew he could. Reuben also wondered if his dad remembered the promise to buy him a horse once he could handle the plow to satisfy his dad.

Before Reuben reached the barn, he saw the other children racing toward him.

"It's ready, it's ready, it's ready!" shouted Jonas and Lizzie Mae. They were stumbling along over the uneven pasture field, half skipping, half jumping, and shouting as they went.

"What's ready?" Reuben called back. The two kept repeating, "It's ready, it's ready, it's ready."

As Reuben drew even with them, he stopped the horses, who were rather skiddish because of the commotion.

"Now, you two settle down. What are you talking about?"

"The books with us in them," Jonas shouted.

"With us?" Reuben looked puzzled.

"Ya, and Mammi and Dawdy (Grandma and Grandpa), and all the uncles and aunts and cousins."

"Oh," guessed Reuben, "you mean the *Maust Family History?*"

"Ya," Mandy replied, "and Mom said my name is in it, too."

"I'm sure it is," agreed Reuben. "You go back to the house now while I unhitch the team. I hope I can get them calmed down after all your yelling."

He also was eager to see what the books contained. But he would wait along with the rest of his family. Sunday was the day for rest and reading. Other days were for work!

17
What Does It Matter?

It was a lazy Sunday afternoon. The Weaver family had returned earlier than usual from church at Abe Yoders, their neighbors. Mom said she was tired and needed to go home.

They changed into more comfortable clothes and prepared to examine the books which had arrived the day before.

"Let me have one," burbled Mandy, reaching out her chubby arms.

"You can't read well enough yet," Reuben told her.

"I know my name, and Mom said it's in there."

"So it is," Lucy assured her. "Come here and I'll show you." Mandy felt important.

"Come on, sis," offered Reuben. "We'll share one." This surprised and pleased Salome. It was special when her brother paid attention to her.

"Everyone needs a story. Here we have many stories about our people," Adam told the family. "We need to learn the faith our ancestors had. If we don't know where we came from, we won't know where we're going."

As they scanned the pages of the *Maust Family History*, Reuben and Salome found many interesting passages in the book. They read of one man who was a deputy mayor.

"Think of that," remarked Salome. "We must be important people to have a relative as a mayor."

"Read a little further, and then see what you think," Reuben suggested.

"I don't see anything out of the ordinary," Salome replied.

"You didn't look far enough, then. Listen to this. 'One Hans Stuben was fined an enormous sum of five gulden and fourteen albuses for hitting Mayor Jessie Maust on the nose.' "

How Reuben and Salome laughed!

"My, I wonder how much money that was," Salome mused.

"I'm sure I don't know. But what I'd like to know is why he hit him in the first place," Reuben responded.

"They were probably ashamed to tell," decided Salome.

Many short paragraphs told of the sufferings of their ancestors because of their faith. Some gave their lives for the gospel they held so dear. This was a sobering thought for young minds, and both Reuben and Salome wondered how great their faith would be under such torture.

They found their own family's name and checked all the details. Then the two skipped over many other short accounts of names, dates of birth, number of children, occupations, and deaths.

Reviewing the history of their family somehow gave both brother and sister a deeper sense of belonging. They felt part of a people who had come out of deep trials and struggles. Now they were putting down their roots in a safe place for future generations.

After a while Reuben laid the book aside and stood up to stretch.

"I'm going for a walk," he stated. "Want to come along, Molasses Face?"

"Where to?" Salome asked.

"Oh, down to the covered bridge and maybe come back by the woods, if I'm not too tired."

"You mean if you're not too lazy," teased his sister.

"You'd better stop or I won't let you come."

"Won't say another word," Salome promised, pressing her lips tightly together.

"That'll be the day, when you won't say a word," chuckled Reuben good-naturedly.

"Ach, come along. But first we ought to tell Mom and Dad where we are going."

"Sure, I was going to."

"Don't stay too long," Adam told his children. "You know chore time is in about an hour."

"Now mind, don't go down that steep bank to the water. You can enjoy the scenery without putting yourselves in danger," Lucy cautioned them.

"Okay, Mom. We'll be careful. Don't worry."

Levi and Lizzie Mae begged to go, but Mother said they needed to stay and play with Mandy and Jonas. She and Dad wanted to take a short nap.

"If you play nicely, this evening I'll pop some corn and make cold lemonade. We can sit on the porch and sing, and I'll even let you stay up a little later tonight," Lucy promised.

"May we pick some songs from the *englisch* book?" asked Lizzie Mae.

"Yes, I guess we can let you do that," Mother replied.

"Oh, goody!"

Reuben and Salome would be home by then, and everyone had such a good time when they sang together. They had recently bought the *englisch* hymnal, and it was fun to try some of the songs they had overheard the young people singing.

Lizzie Mae and Levi coaxed the two other children outside to play tag, blindman's buff, and hide-and-seek.

Meanwhile, Reuben and Salome strolled through the side of the pasture toward the covered bridge.

"Aren't the trees pretty this time of the year?" Salome asked as they walked along the fencerow. Some leaves were already starting to turn bright colors.

"Ya," answered Reuben. "Fall is the best time of the year. Crops are almost all harvested, and the weather is cooler. Next year by this time I'll be *rumschpringing* (going with the youth of the church). I hope I'll get my horse and buggy soon."

"You aren't even sixteen yet," Salome reminded him.

"Almost. Sometimes if a boy is grown-up enough, he gets a rig sooner. Dad told me so."

"Well, I hope you do, then maybe you and I can ride to church together. It gets so crowded in our buggy, and soon there will be a new *Bobbli* (baby)."

"I know," murmured Reuben, rather embarrassed that his sister mentioned it. Maybe that was why his mom wanted to come home from church early.

Pretty butterflies flitted here and there and soft gossamer strands of silky cobwebs crossed their path. A bobwhite whistled his cheery note from the rail fence.

A few leaves floated silently to the ground. A red squirrel scolded from a high branch as though annoyed at being disturbed. In the wonder of it all, the two reached the old covered bridge.

"Listen!" exclaimed Reuben. "I hear someone under there." Standing quietly, they heard voices. As they were about to leave, two of Abe Yoder's boys came out from beneath the bridge."

"Oh, it's you we heard," said Reuben.

"Ya, come on down," they invited.

"Naw, we'd better not. Dad and Mom don't want us to."

"Aw, come on. Lydia is down here with us. If she isn't scared, why should you be?" Joel mocked. "What does it matter?"

"I'm not scared," Reuben answered.

"Prove it, then," Rob Yoder challenged him.

Again Reuben felt the pressure to do like his friends. Against Salome's pleading, Reuben went down the steep bank.

Halfway down, Reuben lost his footing and fell onto a large rock. He could tell right away that he had a bad cut on his right leg.

When the Yoder children saw what happened to Reuben, they left so they wouldn't get in trouble with their own parents. But they didn't realize how badly Reuben was injured.

"Can you climb back up?" asked Salome.

"I'll try. Ouch, this really hurts. Now I wish I hadn't come down here."

"Oh, Reuben, I see you're bleeding! Can I help you some way?"

"Yes, maybe you can get that dead branch over there and hold one end of it down to me. Then I can pull myself up without having to use my sore leg so much."

With some struggle they managed to get Reuben up the bank and they started toward home.

"Can you walk?" asked Salome.

"You must help me," admitted Reuben as he limped a few steps. "Here, I'll break this branch to the right length and use it for a cane. How old and frail I am already!"

Why do I have to prove myself in front of others? he thought. *This is why I have to listen to my parents and use good sense.*

18
That Rock

It was a sad pair who made their way homeward.

"Lean on me, Reuben. I don't mind," Salome kindly offered.

Reuben's trousers were torn and his right leg had an ugly gash which was bleeding profusely. Salome's imagination was running rampant. What if her brother would bleed to death or be a cripple for life, or worse yet, if his leg would fall off! Oh, they must get home. She was half dragging Reuben and thus hindering his progress.

"*Loss los* (let loose)," complained Reuben. "You're pulling on my arm. I can't go faster."

"But I don't want your leg to fall off," wailed Salome.

"*Ach, du bist kindisch* (you're childish)! Maybe you'd better run on home and have Dad come for me with the buggy. I'll sit here in the grass and wait."

"But what if the buzzards come after you?"

"Don't be so silly, just go. *Mach schnell* (hurry)!"

Reuben need not have told his sister to *mach schnell*. She fairly flew across the pasture. Never had he seen her run so fast. Reuben knew that to slow the bleeding he should apply pressure to the wound. He took his clean white handkerchief from his pocket and held it firmly in place over the cut.

Soon Salome reached home and burst through the kitchen door, yelling at the top of her voice, "Dad, Mom, *kumm schnell* (come quickly)."

Her parents had just finished their naps and were in the living room. When they heard her anxious screams, they hurried to the kitchen.

"Was is letz (what's wrong)?" asked Adam.

Lucy clutched at her heart. Such excitement was not good for her.

Gasping for breath, Salome began. "Reuben, his leg's about to fall off. He's waiting for you to bring the buggy, down near the covered bridge."

"Can't he walk?" Adam asked.

"Not very good, unless someone pulls him, and he didn't want me to. I'm afraid the buzzards will get him."

"What happened? Where is he?" Lucy asked, trembling with fright.

"He went down the creek bank because Abe Yoder's boys told him to. They dared him, and he fell and cut his leg almost off. Now he's sitting by the road in the grass waiting for Dad."

"Don't worry," Adam told his wife. "I'll go right away. You know the imagination Salome has. It probably isn't that bad."

The rest of the Weaver children heard their sister's

screams and came indoors to see what happened. Lucy fetched some clean white rags, Black Diamond Liniment, and salve. She would be prepared when Adam and Reuben returned.

Meanwhile, Salome corralled the younger children and in the most descriptive manner related to them the incident leading to Reuben's injury. Mandy covered her eyes as if to shut out the gory details. Jonas began to cry. Levi and Lizzie Mae just looked at her and listened in shocked silence.

"Stop it," protested Lizzie Mae. "Now you make the little one so afraid. I bet Reuben will be alright and Dad will chase those old buzzards away."

"You just wait and see if he isn't hurt bad," pronounced Salome, tilting her head importantly.

Jonas ran to his mother. "Mom, Salome says Reuben is real bad hurt. I don't want his leg to fall off, and I don't want any old birds to get him."

"Ei-yi-yi-yi!" exclaimed Lucy. "That Salome is telling you things, and she makes them worse all the time. Salome, come here. . . ."

Lucy pulled Salome off to the side and told her separately, "I want you to stop talking to the other children about what happened. We'll know soon enough how hurt he is. I'm sure you're upset, but usually things aren't as bad as we expect. Go and wash Mandy's face and change her dress. The children must have been playing in the sandbox. Now mind, no more talking about Reuben."

Lucy herself was anxious, but she would not give in to her worries. She wanted to keep the youngsters from panic and be ready to help her injured son.

113

As the wheels of the buggy rattled over the stones in the driveway, Lucy and her children gathered on the porch. They watched in silence as Adam jumped down and Levi rushed out to tie Star to the hitching post. Lucy wondered why Reuben just sat there. Was he really hurt that badly?

"Come on," said Adam. "I'll give you a hand."

Reuben slowly climbed from the buggy and leaned on his father for support. Lucy tried to suppress a gasp. She observed the torn and bloody pant leg and how slowly her son limped toward the house. Well, they must take care of him right now. Lucy rolled up her sleeves and began to take charge.

"Salome, bring a kitchen chair to the porch for Reuben. Mandy, get my scissors from the sewing machine drawer. Jonas, bring the wash basin with clean cool water and some soap. I'll get my bandages and other supplies."

Everyone scurried to their tasks. When one family member was in need, they all rallied around. Reuben could barely make the steps leading to the porch. There were only three, but it seemed like an impossible chore.

"How bad is it?" Lucy asked her husband.

"Bad enough," answered Adam, "but we can take care of it. You're a good nurse, and I'm sure it will heal."

"Looks to me like we'll need to get the crutches down from the attic," said Lucy after thoroughly washing, treating, and dressing Reuben's leg.

"Ya, I'm afraid so," replied Reuben.

"Why did you do it, Son?" Lucy asked.

"Well, they dared me to come down the bank, and besides, Abe's boys were playing down there, and so was their sister. I didn't see what harm it could do. If it weren't for that rock, it wouldn't have happened."

"No, Reuben. If you would have obeyed your parents, it wouldn't have happened."

"Well, I guess, but can't a fellow have any fun?"

"Wasn't the walk with your sister fun?"

"Ya, but I thought it would be more fun to play with Rob and Joel."

"Dad and I have been wondering if your weakness of giving in to other young folks might someday get you into serious trouble."

"I'll try to do better," Reuben murmured.

Because of all the excitement, they were late in tending the animals. Reuben couldn't do his chores, so Levi and Jonas had more work to do to make up for that.

After the supper dishes were done, Salome said, "Let's sing tonight, Mom."

"Yes, let's," Lizzie Mae joined in.

"Alright, I believe we will," Lucy agreed. "Things always seem to go better when we sing."

They pulled out the *englisch* hymnal and leafed through to find some songs they knew. Reuben smiled a bit as the first two songs chosen were "Rock of Ages" and "Lead Me to the Rock." He was glad they referred to a Rock of healing.

For the next two weeks, Reuben was the center of attention. His brothers and sisters were at his beck and call. He had to miss the first week of school, and when he did start, he couldn't play ball the first few days.

Yet he found it embarrassing when someone asked

how his injury happened. He knew he had made a mistake, and he was resolved to do better. But he didn't want to talk about it more than necessary. Usually he just shrugged his shoulders and replied, "I slipped on the riverbank."

Sometimes he laughed and said, "I met a rock, and we got too close!"

19
The Horse Sale

Christmastime had arrived and along with it two weeks of vacation from school. The Weaver children were ready for a change.

Salome and Lizzie Mae knew there would be cleaning, baking, quilt piecing, comfort knotting, and various other tasks. But they enjoyed the excitement of the holiday season, and Lucy counted these projects as part of their education.

Reuben and Levi would be kept busy cleaning the horse stables and cow shed, repairing and oiling harnesses, and making sure the outbuildings were in order and tight for the winter. There were always cobwebs to sweep somewhere.

Christmas in an Amish home is a happy time even if it is different from the celebrations of their *englisch* neighbors. Yet as everywhere, routines and traditions build on memories from the past and enrich the present.

"We'll be making candy soon," Salome told Reuben on the way home from school. "You boys have to work in the smelly old barn while we girls get to do the good part of Christmas."

"Oh no, you don't," Reuben reminded her. "The good part is eating the candy, cookies, and cakes. We boys are experts at that!"

"You sure are," agreed Salome. "You would eat it almost faster than we can make it if you were allowed in the kitchen."

"Someone *ought* to taste it to make sure it's fit to eat," Reuben teased.

"Don't you worry. I haven't seen you throw any away."

"I'll wash your face for that," declared Reuben. He started running after his sister with a handful of snow, but she kept ahead of him.

"What are you two up to now?" asked Lucy as her youngsters burst through the doorway, their cheeks glowing red from the outdoor cold and the exercise.

"We were only teasing and having some fun on our way home," Reuben told his mother.

"Well, stomp that snow from your boots before you track it further in the house."

Reuben stepped back on the mat and removed his four-buckle boots.

"Where are Levi and the others?" asked Lucy.

"They're walking with the Yoder children. We told them to come, but they were throwing snowballs."

"Throwing," remarked Lucy, as she saw the stragglers come down the lane. "I'd say it looks more like they rolled in the stuff. Salome, take the broom once and go outside and sweep them off."

Lucy could not help but smile at the sparkling eyes of her children. She remembered the days when she too was excited about Christmas and school vacation.

After chores and supper, the dishes were cleared and washed. Then Reuben and Salome were ready to page through the wish book, as they called it. That was a mail-order catalog, and it held ever so many wonderful things.

"I wonder why we can't have pretty decorations in our windows like the *Englischer* have," Salome remarked to Reuben.

"Ya, and a Christmas tree with lights and shiny stuff all over it."

"Maybe it's all for fancy," Salome speculated.

"Wonder what we'll get for Christmas," Reuben said.

"Perhaps a *goldich Nixli* (golden nothing)," Lucy joked, "unless you come and help pick out these nutmeats."

"Do we have to, Mom?" Salome asked.

"If you want walnut fudge, hickory nut cake, and other candies, come Christmas."

The children had helped gather nuts in the fall. Father had hulled them, Mother helped him crack the shells, and now they would remove the meats with nut picks. Even the smaller children helped.

"Dad, why don't we have decorations and Christmas trees like *englisch* people?" asked Salome.

"Well, there's danger of paying too much attention to those things and forgetting that Christmas is for the birthday of Jesus."

"But it looks so pretty in the stores and windows of houses," Lizzie Mae remarked.

"Pretty isn't always right," stated Adam, and that settled it.

Later that evening and just before bedtime, Adam opened another subject. "Reuben, you'll be sixteen now in a week. What say, since you're out for vacation this Friday and. . . . Well, maybe it wouldn't work," Adam said thoughtfully.

"What, Dad, what wouldn't work?"

"It so happens that this is the Friday for the horse sale, but then you may want to stay home and help with candy making and baking."

"Ach, Dad, you know I want to go to the sale more than anything. The girls always help Mom. Can't I go, Dad?"

"Salome told me you thought someone should taste their goodies. Are you sure you want to give up that job?"

"No, Dad, I was only kidding. I'm sure the candy and cookies will all be good. They always are. Please . . . let me go to the sale."

Adam thought he had strung his son along enough. He liked a bit of fun himself, but he didn't want to torture him.

"Ya, I guess it's time we buy a horse for you, Reuben. I watched you work all summer and fall. You did well and I'm pleased."

"Did I plow straight furrows?"

"Ya, you did," laughed Adam. "You're a good cornhusker, too. I can hardly keep ahead of you. Now if only you can keep from being influenced by other young folks when they dare you. . . ."

"Dad, I'll try real hard. I don't want to be one of the outback bunch at singings."

"I would hope not. We expect you to go inside and help sing. That's what singings are for."

The outback bunch were a few boys and even some girls who stayed outside at singings and tried to disrupt those who went inside to sing. Reuben knew about that from the singing that was held at their place.

Lucy was listening to this exchange and had her own counsel to add. "Reuben, I hope you don't choose such a fast horse. Adam, try to make sure it's one that's safe."

"Now, Lucy, don't fret and worry on account of this," her husband replied. "We'll use good judgment."

Well, thought Reuben, *there goes my chance to have a horse named Prince. I'll have to settle for a mare for my first horse to satisfy Mom.*

Salome thought Reuben was very grown-up to be getting his own rig. Levi begged to go along, too, but Dad said, "No, this is Reuben's day."

On Friday morning Reuben was up bright and early and did his chores with zest. The ride to the sale barn seemed endless, but finally they were there. Father found good seats, and after greeting many friends, settled down to do business.

Horse after horse entered the ring and was auctioned off, but none caught Reuben's fancy. Neither had Adam found anything to his liking.

"Let's go for a bite to eat," Adam proposed. "It's almost twelve-thirty."

Reuben hated to leave the ring. What if the horse he

had been waiting for would sell while they went to lunch?

"Don't worry. There are plenty to choose from. If we don't find one today, there are more sales," his dad assured him.

However, Reuben had his heart set on buying one today. He kept looking around.

"There she is, Dad!" Reuben exclaimed as they made their way past the box stalls. "That's my horse!"

"Wait a minute," said Adam. "She's not yours yet. I want to look at this mare first and know something about her record."

"But Dad, what if they sell her while we're at lunch? I don't want to miss this chance."

"She's number twenty-two, and they're only selling fifteen now. We'll be back in time."

Reuben never ate so fast in his life. Horse sales were so exciting.

20
My Horse, My Friend

Adam took time to visit with friends after they finished lunch.

"Come on, Dad," Reuben urged him. "Let's get back in the stands."

"So," said Alvin Hoffman, "you must have a boy who likes to watch horses sell."

"Actually, we are looking to buy one," Adam told him.

"Ready for *Rumschpringe* (running around with the young folks)?" Alvin asked.

"He is sixteen now and a good worker," Adam stated with satisfaction.

"I see he's chomping at the bit to get back to the auctioning, so I won't keep you," laughed Alvin.

Reuben was grateful for Alvin's consideration.

"Dad, let's not stop and talk to anyone now, or we might be late," Reuben begged.

"Reuben, we must never be so busy or hurried that

we don't have time for others."

"But can't we just say *wie geht's?* (how do you do?) and go on?"

"We can, but we need to learn patience, too. Maybe you're not ready for a horse of your own if you put that first."

The very thought of having to wait overwhelmed Reuben. "I'd never do that, Dad. Mom and you and the family are more important than any horse."

Yet in his heart Reuben knew the horse would run a close second. He knew he would have to watch himself if he was going to put family and friends first.

What a relief to see the stall which contained the horse he wanted was not empty. The mare looked at Reuben and pushed her nose over for a snack. Reuben had brought along a carrot just for this purpose, and he fed it to her on his outstretched palm.

"So this is the one you want?" Adam asked as he stopped for a closer inspection.

"This is the one," Reuben answered.

The mare didn't look exactly like the one Reuben had dreamed of for so long, yet he liked this one best.

"What do you see in this horse? Why pick this one instead of another?"

"Oh, I just like her. The color, the way she stands with head held high. She looks like she has spirit. And see how friendly she is. She ate right out of my hand, and she's asking for more."

"We'll wait until they bring her in the ring before we decide," Adam stated. "We need to see her walk around and how she handles herself with people all around. We don't want a skittish horse."

Reuben had already made up his mind. No doubt about it, this was his horse.

They went back to take seats at the auction ring. Two more horses were sold, and then the moment Reuben was waiting for finally arrived. Reuben moved to the edge of his seat. He listened to every word. This mare had a good track record.

"She comes from a good bloodline," announced the auctioneer.

Reuben watched as she was trotted around the arena in front of them. Her black coat glistened, her head remained high, and she trotted with perfect rhythm. She didn't seem to be bothered by the crowd at all.

"Anyone interested who would like to further examine this horse, step into the ring," offered the caretaker.

Adam and two other men made their way out of the stands. Reuben's dad ran his hand over her withers and checked her teeth. He examined her hooves. Even if she was a mare, Reuben still wanted her. He watched Father's face to see if he was pleased. It was hard to tell. Finally the men returned to their places and the bidding began.

"Are you satisfied with her, Dad?"

"Ya. I'll bid on this one."

Reuben's fists clenched tightly and his knuckles showed white as the price increased. He wondered how much his dad was willing to pay.

Reuben saw that Raymond Plank had dropped out of the bidding. That left his Dad and Aaron Lapp. Reuben also noticed that Mrs. Lapp kept shaking her head no each time Aaron bid.

Finally, Adam hesitated, and as Reuben held his breath, he heard the words "going once, going twice, going three times. Sold to Aaron Lapp."

If Reuben had been a child, he would have cried. As far as he was concerned, the sale was over.

"Let's stick around a little while," said Adam. "Maybe we'll see something else we like."

Reuben's heart was not in it any more. What made matters worse was the fact that Aaron's son would be driving this horse to Sunday services and singings, and Reuben would see her all the time. The Lapps and Weavers were in the same church district.

Reuben was relieved when Adam told his son, "Come on. It's time to go home."

Perhaps, thought Reuben, *I was too determined to have her. Maybe Dad is right, that I would have spent too much time with my horse. But, oh, she was just about like the one I wanted for so long!*

Adam saw the dejected look on his son's face and suggested, "You can drive Star until we find a horse for you."

"Ya," responded Reuben slowly. "I know the price was going too high, Dad. I'll try to be *zufridda* (satisfied)."

"God will bless you for that attitude, Reuben. I know you're disappointed, but I'm thankful you don't whine. What do you say, shall we stop by the lunch stand for some hot chocolate? It's pretty chilly, and we have a few miles' drive before we get home."

"There you are," Aaron Lapp said as he sidled up next to Adam at the counter. "I've been looking all over for you."

Reuben wondered if he had come to gloat. Then he was ashamed of such a thought.

"Well, *do bin ich* (here I am)," returned Adam.

"I'll get right to the point," Aaron told him. "*Die Fraa* (the wife) is unhappy with my purchase. She's afraid the mare I bought may be too high-strung for our boy to handle. But I hear Reuben is really good with horses. So if you're willing to pay what I gave, I'll let you have her. You know we have to keep the women happy if we want any *Ruh* (rest)," Aaron laughed.

Reuben couldn't believe his ears. What would his Dad say? *Don't let him say no,* he thought. *Don't let me be disappointed again.*

"*Was saagst du* (what do you say), Reuben?" his father asked. "It would be your horse."

Adam saw the eager look in Reuben's eyes, and he knew how he would answer.

"You know I want that horse, but whatever you decide is best," he replied.

That pleased Adam. "Let's go back to the clerk and make the transaction then," Adam stated.

After they left the clerk with the bill of sale, they made their way through the crowd to their buggy.

"We'll stop on the way home and see if Erkel can come and get her with his horse trailer," Adam told Reuben.

"Can I stay with her until he comes?" Reuben asked.

"No, you'd better come along home and help chore. Remember, you have to get a stall ready for her."

"Oh, I will, Dad. Do you think I should put her next to Star?"

"No, I would put her beside old Mol. She's gentler.

127

But now, Reuben, we can't just call the horse *her*. Since she'll be your horse, it's your job to pick a name. What do you say?"

"I was going to call my horse Prince, but now I can't. You don't call a mare Prince," laughed Reuben.

"Why not Princess, then?" suggested Adam.

"That fits her just fine," agreed Reuben. "She's beautiful with her black color, white blaze, and four white feet. Ya, Princess it is. But whatever I call her, she's my horse, my friend."

"Always take good care of her, and don't race her," his dad advised him.

Reuben could hardly wait to tell his brothers and sisters that at last he had a horse of his own. Now he really felt like a man!

21
The Horse Race

Reuben was the envy of almost every boy in the Amish settlement, although they were all taught not to be envious. It was hard for him not to feel proud as he drove to church or singings with Princess and his new open buggy. Pride was also *verbodde* (forbidden). The bishop said so.

Regularly on Saturdays Reuben washed and polished his buggy until the black paint shone. He groomed Princess and kept her harness oiled. Everything was in top-notch condition.

On the way to church, Reuben would put Princess through her paces. Salome rode with him, and they felt like they were on top of the world.

Winter finally gave way to spring, and seeding time kept them busy in the fields, working from dawn to dusk. But then after seeding and before haying, the young folks gathered for their first ball game of the season. Their practice was to play ball every other

Wednesday evening in the waning light.

"How fast can she run?" Simeon Mullet asked as Reuben untied Princess to go home.

"I don't know. I never tried her," Reuben answered.

"Why not? Are you afraid to race her?"

"Yeah, why don't we see what she can do?" suggested Nate Wagler. "My horse against yours."

"No," replied Reuben, "Dad told me not to race her."

"Aw, come on. You're sixteen, aren't you? Do you still let your old man tell you what to do?"

Reuben resented the way Nate spoke of his father. "My dad's not an old man, and I just don't want to get into trouble," Reuben answered.

"Who's to tell?" asked Willy Chupp. "I'd race if I were you. Sissy, that's what you are!"

Reuben saw that Willy was getting wound up, and that generally set everyone else going and made things worse.

"I think I'll just go on home," Reuben said. Yet he was tantalized by the opportunity to show what his horse could do.

The game had gone well, without any arguments, and Reuben wanted it to end that way. But the jeers and taunts of his peers were getting to him.

"Come on," urged Willy, jumping into the buggy with Reuben. "Let's go."

Reuben knew he shouldn't, but once again he gave in to temptation. He was sure that Princess was the best horse, but he wanted the other boys to know that too.

"*Just this once*," he declared emphatically. "After this,

I don't want to hear any more. You understand?"

"Boy, listen who's giving the orders around here. Guess because he has a Princess, he thinks he's king," mocked Nate.

Two of the boys came over to Reuben and quietly advised him to ignore his tormentors, but he felt he must prove himself.

"How far do you want to race?" Reuben asked.

"You name it, and I'll beat you there," Nate answered.

"How about across the bridge to the mill and back?"

"Okay, to the sawmill it is," agreed Nate. "Get ready to eat my dust."

"Willy, I wish you'd get off my buggy," Reuben said. "I don't want anything to happen to you, and your weight will hold me back."

"No. If you make me get off, I'll tell that you raced," Willy threatened.

"Hold on, then," sighed Reuben.

"Pull up even, and I'll tell you when to start," Simeon Mullet ordered.

"Ready, go!" and they were off. Some of the boys ran down the road to watch as well as they could. A cloud of dust blocked their view.

Reuben kept a slight check on Princess until they neared the bridge. He knew it was too narrow for two buggies, so he gave Princess full rein and urged her on, expecting to make it across ahead of Nate. His timing was wrong, and Nate pulled alongside him, crowding his rig against the railing.

There was a crunching, grinding sound as Princess lurched forward. Willy was thrown out over the embankment and into the shallow water below. Both buggies stopped in the entanglement.

Reuben steadied his horse and then rushed down the bank. Nate stood dumbfounded on the bridge, holding both horses.

"Willy," shouted Reuben, "Willy, are you hurt?"

He lay so still. Reuben turned him face up.

"Nate, oh Nate, Willy's gone. He's dead! What have we done? We need to get help, Nate."

Both boys were shocked and subdued. Reuben dragged Willy onto the grass at the edge of the stream and checked him for vital signs. There were none.

"You want to stay here with the horses while I go back and send some of the boys for help?" Reuben asked.

"No," replied Nate, "I don't like to see Willy lying down there. You stay, and I'll go back."

"Well, hurry," Reuben demanded.

Nate took off running.

"What will I tell Dad?" Reuben said aloud. "And what's more, how can I tell Willy's parents? Oh, I know I didn't want him to ride along, but I should not have raced in the first place. Why does it matter so much to me what others say?"

Then Reuben prayed as he had never prayed before.

It seemed hours before help came. Word spread fast, though, and many neighbors and church members gathered at the scene and also at the Chupp home.

Reuben's dad unhitched Princess and pulled the mangled buggy to the side of the road. They would come for it later. They tied Princess behind Adam's buggy and started for home. Not much was said on the way.

"I've got to talk to you, Dad," confided Reuben that evening. "I can't sleep if I don't. Dad, it's all my fault. You told me not to race Princess, and I did. I did because some of the boys were name-calling again. Oh, Dad, I wish I hadn't done it." Reuben released a sob.

"How did Willy get to be in this?" Adam asked.

"He begged to ride in my buggy. I told him to get out, but he wouldn't. Nate and I locked wheels on the bridge, and it threw Willy out. I'm to blame for this," Reuben admitted.

When Salome heard the story, she felt sorry for her brother. She knew he was hurting deeply.

Lucy, too, was shocked and grieving with both Reuben and the Chupp family. She wondered if this was what it would take to bring the young folks closer together and in obedience to their parents and the church.

One of the hardest things Reuben ever did was to face Willy's parents and assist as one of the pallbearers. He was comforted somewhat when Mrs. Chupp said kindly, laying her hand on his shoulder, "Reuben, don't brood over this. You didn't want Willy to ride along. Willy's mind was different from other boys. I don't think he was accountable for many things he did. He's in a better place now."

Reuben nodded, but he couldn't speak.

For two months after the accident, Reuben didn't go to singings, ball games, or any other activities the young folks had.

"Why don't you go to singing?" asked Salome on Sunday evening.

"I just don't feel like it anymore," Reuben answered.

"Well, I hope you will go before too long. I'll soon be ready for *Rumschpringe*."

"What? You—ready to go with the young folks! I can't believe it, Molasses Face," Reuben exclaimed with a grin.

It was the first that Salome had seen her brother grin for some time, and it made her feel real good.

"Ya, my birthday will be in three weeks, and I'll be fifteen. Mom says I can go when I'm sixteen."

"I'll have to get all spiffed up to take such a pretty girl with me," said Reuben.

Salome made a face at him, but she knew he would be her fun-loving brother again. She was happy.

22
On My Own Feet

A year later when Salome turned sixteen, her parents gave her permission to go to singings.

"Come on, Molasses Face," teased Reuben. "If you want to ride with me, you'd better be on time."

"What's your hurry, Reuben?" asked his mother.

"I like to get a good seat. Sometimes I'm asked to be a *Vorsinger* (song leader), so I need better lighting. The gas lamps are usually placed above the table where the main singers sit."

"It's good to know you help with singing and don't go with the outback bunch," Adam remarked.

"Ach, Dad, I wouldn't," Reuben assured him.

"I'm ready," Salome said, slipping into a light home-made jacket.

"Tie your bonnet strings," Lucy instructed her daughter.

"Ach, Mom, do I have to?" objected Salome.

"You don't want your bonnet to fly off, do you?"

asked Lucy. "Princess runs too fast, and it makes wind."

Reuben smiled at his mother's words. He was still pleased with his horse's speed even though there was an undercurrent of sadness from the accident that took Willy's life. That experience seemed to have given him several extra years of maturity.

"Don't stay too late," Adam told his son and daughter. "Tomorrow's a workday."

"We'll be back in good time, Dad, unless Salome gives me trouble," Reuben answered as he held the door for Salome.

His sister elbowed him in fun as she went past him, and all the younger children came out on the porch to see them off.

The drive to singing was enjoyable and uneventful. How Reuben loved to watch the ripple of muscle underneath the smooth, almost blue-black coat of Princess as she ran, never breaking stride. What a horse!

He doubted if even the one he had seen in the magazine could hold a candle to her. When he thought of the magazine, he remembered Willy and that fateful night. He became very quiet.

"A penny for your thoughts," said Salome.

"What?" asked Reuben, for he had been in a world of his own.

"I said, a penny for your thoughts. You seemed miles away."

"Ach, Salome, I can't forget the night Willy was killed. Somehow I still blame myself. Do you think it would help if I'd join church?"

"Maybe. Why don't you ask Dad what he thinks?"

"Ya, that's what I'll do. I'll ask Dad," agreed Reuben.

After a minute of silence, Salome asked, "How should I act tonight?"

"What do you mean?"

"It's my first time at singing, and I'm nervous. What if I do something wrong, and the others laugh at me?"

"You sure seemed anxious enough to come," Reuben reminded her.

"Ya, I wanted to, but what if I can't sing nice? And do I sit at the table or just on one of the separate benches?"

"Why not sit with your friends you usually chum with? Whatever you do, don't whisper and giggle like some do," her brother cautioned.

"Oh, my, no! I wouldn't," exclaimed Salome.

"I believe Polly Kuhns and Lizabet Raber do it to get the boys' attention. I think they're *kindisch* (childish)," Reuben commented.

"Well, at least you noticed them! *I* sure don't want any boys' attention!" Salome declared.

"Oh no?" remarked Reuben. "Are you sure? I've seen Ray Danny's Mosie look at you more than once at church."

"No, you haven't. You're just teasing me." But Salome blushed a deep pink.

"Your face is turning red. Are you sure you haven't made sheep's eyes at him?" Reuben laughed.

"Stop it, now. You know I'm too young to think seriously about *Buwe* (boys)."

She was glad Reuben could laugh again, and she liked just a bit of kidding, but she wouldn't admit that to her brother.

They were nearing the Yoder home where the singing was being held this evening, and Salome did not want to arrive with a red face.

"How do I look?" she asked Reuben as she rubbed her cheeks and straightened her clothes.

"You look alright to me." Reuben had the urge to tell her that she was still blushing, but he restrained himself.

"I'll let you off by the summerhouse. That's where the girls leave their wraps, isn't it?"

"Ya," replied Salome soberly. "Oh, Reuben, I'm so scared."

"Don't be. There's no need for it. See, there are some girls ready to go in now."

The girls looked as Reuben's rig pulled up the driveway. Two of them waved.

"Why, it's Mabel and Dora," giggled Salome as she waved back. "I hope they wait for me."

"They will," Reuben assured her. He knew Mabel and Dora were good friends with his sister.

As he dropped Salome by the gate to the summerhouse, Reuben said, "I'll let you know when I'm ready to go home."

"Alright," responded Salome, tripping lightly down the walk to her friends.

Everything seemed to be just perfect. The young folks sang with such gusto that it filled the house.

Then chaos broke loose. The door to the kitchen opened, and some of the group who were outside came in, dragging the family dog along. Shep was barking loudly in protest.

Next someone released two chickens in the kitchen.

They were frightened and flew about squawking wild-ly. One of the hens landed on Edna Stauffer's hand. She screamed, and feathers wafted across the table. Such a commotion!

Singing soon broke up. Salome was sad that it had to end as it did. The boys went for their buggies and picked up their sisters or girlfriends in front of the house.

"Reuben, does this often happen?" she asked as they made their way home.

"No," sighed her brother. "Tonight was extra bad. Granted, there are usually a few who won't come in-side at all or who straggle in late. But I've never known them to disrupt us like they did tonight. It's too bad it had to happen at all, but especially on your first night at the singing. Maybe you don't want to come any-more."

"Oh yes, I do. They didn't act up that much when singing was at our place."

As they neared the bridge where the accident had occurred, Reuben's mind once more turned to Willy, and the old feelings of guilt seemed overwhelming. Why, oh, why hadn't he obeyed his father? Why had he let a dare make such a difference?

He would talk to his dad about taking instruction to make a confession of faith at baptism and be received as a member of the church. Perhaps he would do bet-ter then.

Monday morning Reuben approached his father.

"Dad, if you have a minute, I'd like to ask you a question," he started.

"A minute I've got, but not much else," Adam remarked. He noticed the solemn look on his son's face. "What is it, Reuben?"

"I can't seem to forget that because I disobeyed and raced Princess, that accident happened and Willy is gone. Do you think, if I joined church, that I wouldn't feel so guilty? Sometimes I hardly sleep all night."

"Reuben," Adam began kindly, "we cannot change the past. Willy's parents have said they don't blame you. What you did was wrong, but we have forgiven you. God also forgives, if we but ask, as we do in the Lord's Prayer.

"Perhaps you can take this as a teaching experience to help you stand on your own feet. Your mother and I will be happy to have you become a member of the church, but not just to ease your conscience. First you must forgive yourself and learn to be a man. When others jeer at you, stand on your own feet."

Reuben determined within his heart to do exactly that. *On my own feet,* he said to himself.

23
A Victory Won

Reuben did not realize how soon he would need to put into practice the advice of his father. Nor did he realize how hard it would be—even impossible on his own.

The family was relaxing one Saturday evening after chores and supper. The few stores in town usually closed at six o'clock. Tonight the local general store was running a sale and would remain open until nine.

"Dad," said Reuben, "is it alright if I go into town for the sale at Jackson's store? I need some shaving cream, shoestrings, work gloves, and a few other things."

"Well, normally I'd say no, but since tomorrow is our between Sunday, I guess you can go."

On a Saturday evening before church, various activities would be put aside so all would be rested and alert during preaching. But services were held every other Sunday, and it was not their district's turn to have services that Sunday.

"Oh, Mom, may I go with Reuben? I could use a few things myself," begged Salome.

"Now what would you need that's so important it can't wait?" asked Lucy.

"Toothpaste, for one thing, and hairpins. And now's a good time to buy while they're on sale," she reminded her mother. Salome knew that if there was a chance to buy things at a reduced price, she was more likely to get her mother's permission.

"Ach, my, I don't know. It's not *kauscher* (proper) for young girls to be seen in town on Saturday evenings. I've heard say that just the wild ones go then," mother commented.

"Let her come, Mom," Reuben said, much to Salome's surprise. "I'll take good care of her. Besides, I'd be glad for her company."

"*Was denkst du* (what do you think)?" Lucy asked her husband.

"If you promise to stay out of trouble and come straight home, I will let you both go this time," Adam replied.

Salome fairly flew upstairs to get ready. How grateful she was to her parents and to Reuben. Ever since the accident, a special bond had formed between brother and sister.

"Come on, Molasses Face," Reuben called. "Let's get going before they close the store." Salome knew he was teasing, but she hurried just the same.

"Tie your bonnet strings, Salome, and use the lap robe if it gets chilly," Lucy advised.

"Ach, Mom, I'm no *Bobbli* (baby)," her daughter said.

"Reuben, don't drive Princess too fast. Be sure you are home by nine-thirty. That should give you plenty of time."

"Ya, Dad, I will not drive Princess fast, and we will be home before it's late."

Lucy knew she wouldn't rest easy until her family was all safely in their beds for the night. The parents sat on the porch and watched as their two oldest children drove out the lane and turned down the road toward town.

"Mom," commented Adam, "we have to let go some time. They're growing up, and I hope we have taught them well enough to be able to trust them."

"Yes, Adam, but you know how Reuben struggles so when other young folks tempt him."

"He did have a real problem with that, Lucy, but since Willy Chupp's death, I see a difference. He has never forgiven himself for what happened," Adam told his wife.

"I know," Lucy said. "That hurt look in his eyes at times—it seems he's miles away. It's something none of us can forget. But, oh, I wish I could help him."

"He even asked if I think it would help for him to join the church."

"Did he really? Well, what did you say?"

"I told him we'd be happy to have him be baptized and become a member, but not just to ease his mind. We had a long talk, and I think he's trying to forgive himself."

Meanwhile, Reuben and Salome were thoroughly enjoying the ride in the cool of the evening. They sang part of the time and also just talked.

"I'm going to buy some candy for the rest of the family if I have enough money," Salome said.

"I'd help, but are you sure it would reach home? Or would you eat it all on the way?" laughed Reuben.

"You know *I* wouldn't." Salome gave her brother a friendly push. "But I don't know if I can keep it away from you."

"Look," observed Reuben as they neared the hitching posts. "Mom was right. There are the troublemakers. Well, we'll go about our business and pretend not to notice them."

That was rather hard to do since the rowdy gang was right there where Reuben needed to tie up Princess.

"Hey, look who's here," Nate Wagler announced loudly.

"Ya," added Simeon Mullet, "and he even brought a *schee Meedel* (pretty girl) along."

Salome looked straight ahead.

"Come on," said Reuben, after tying Princess. "Let's go, Salome."

"Oh, so you don't talk to ordinary people," scoffed one of the loafers.

Reuben looked surprised to find Willy Chupp's younger brother lounging at the curb with Nate and Simeon.

"What are you doing here, Harley?" Reuben asked.

"Just hanging around with the others," he answered.

"Ya," said Nate, "he knows who to go with for fun. We're good buddies."

Reuben didn't answer but made his way toward

Jackson's store. He felt almost sick to his stomach to think that Nate and Simeon would get Harley to run with their group.

Probably a half-dozen boys were loitering by the hitchrack. Most of them just laughed at the remarks Nate and Simeon made.

"I wish we didn't need to go back to the hitching bar," confided Salome after making her purchases.

"Aw, don't worry. Chances are the boys aren't there anymore," Reuben tried to assure her. "If they are, I could get the rig and pick you up a block away."

"No," said Salome. "I'm going to stay with you. I just wish they wouldn't heckle us so."

But the guys were there and waiting with a plan to distract them.

"Hey, Reuben," challenged Nate, "we boys are going to play a little pool at the pool hall. We don't play for a lot of money. Why don't you leave your sister with Effie and Mattie and join us? The girls can do some window shopping until we're done."

"No," said Reuben. "I promised Dad we wouldn't stay late."

"Oh, a sissy, Daddy's good boy!" Nate mocked. He seemed to be the ringleader.

"Call it what you will," said Reuben as he shrugged his shoulders, "but I'm going home."

Effie and Mattie giggled and whispered as Salome walked by them on her way to the buggy. Then Effie called out, "Come on, Salome, let's look around town a little. Let Reuben have some fresh air."

"Ach, let them go," said Harley, "they're too goody-goody."

"Yeah," remarked Simeon, "yellow is what I call it. Reuben knows he can't win 'cause he doesn't know how to play. Afraid to try, I bet!"

Reuben felt the old temptation rising within to prove himself. "Oh yeah," he retorted, "well, I just bet I could if I wanted to."

"Show us, then," Nate challenged him.

"Reuben, don't," pleaded Salome.

Reuben once again struggled, but this time he remembered his father's words: "Stand on your own feet. Be a man."

"I have better things to do," Reuben finally declared. He slowly untied his horse and started on the way home.

"Yellow, sissy" came the taunts as they left. "Afraid you'll lose. Tied to your sister's apron strings."

As they drove out of town, Salome said, "I'm proud of you, Reuben. You won a victory this time."

That made it all worthwhile.

24
No Greater Love

Reuben knew he must act quickly. It was wheat threshing time and the big outfit was at Roman Chupps. The field they were harvesting lay on the other side of the railroad tracks.

Harley Chupp's wagon was loaded with sheaves and ready to take to the threshing machine. It was time for the two-forty-five flyer passenger train.

Reuben could hear the whistle of the big locomotive in the distance.

"Hey, Harley," yelled Nate Wagler, "I'll bet if you hurry with your load, you can beat that train."

Nate and many other boys were helping in the usual threshing ring. Some of the boys were pitching sheaves onto the horse-drawn wagons. Others stacked them, and still others were drivers.

"You think so?" asked Harley.

"Sure you can. Make 'em run," urged Nate, referring to the sorrels Harley was driving.

The idea struck fear into the rest of the boys. Even Simeon Mullet, who generally agreed with Nate, protested.

"No, Harley," he said. "Don't try it."

"Aw, come on," Nate urged, "the longer you wait the closer that train gets."

"Stop," yelled Reuben, "you can't make it."

"Prove them wrong," Nate shouted.

Harley slapped the lines smartly across the horses' backs, and they took off running. The sheaves of grain bounced around, and the load shifted. Several men working the far side of the field looked in astonishment at the careening wagon.

As Harley got the team going, they became excited and wild. Harley couldn't have stopped them if he had wanted to.

"A runaway," remarked Atlee Kaufman.

"Ya, and the train is coming. I just hope whoever is driving that team can turn them away from the crossing."

"It looks like Roman Chupp's outfit," Joel Kuhn observed.

Reuben had been pitching sheaves for Abe Yoder's boy. Now as he saw the Chupp team running with the loaded wagon and saw the train approaching, he realized that Harley couldn't beat the train. Reuben went into action.

Quickly he jumped on Abe's wagon and shouted at the driver, Abe's son Freddie, to scoot off. He grabbed the lines and took a shortcut across the field toward a spot in front of the crossing toward which Harley and his team were headed. Abe's wagon had not even half a load, but dodging the standing wheat shocks wasn't easy.

"Please, God," he prayed, "help me make it in time."

Then all he could think of was the *Unser Vater* (Our Father) prayer, and he said it over and over. "Our Father which art in heaven." He dwelt on the part "deliver us from evil."

All work in the field came to an abrupt halt as everyone anxiously looked on. The train whistled for the crossing as it came closer.

"What's that Adam Weaver's boy doing?" asked Atlee Kaufman.

"I thought he had more *Verschtand* (sense) than running those horses. You would think he would have learned his lesson from the accident with Chupp's older son."

"*Es guckt mir* (it looks to me) as if he is trying to stop Roman's team," answered Joel Kuhn.

"Ei-yi-yi-yi! I hope he makes it. There's going to be a crash, that's for sure!"

Reuben drove those horses for all they were worth. Harley was getting close to the crossing, and so was the train.

Reuben laid one more hard lash on the horses' backs and pulled directly in front of Harley's team and wagon. "Whoa," he yelled as he pulled back on the reins as hard as he could. His team skidded to a stop, blocking the Chupp sorrels.

The train whistled shrilly, and Harley's horses veered so they wouldn't hit Reuben's wagon. Then they reared, bringing their front hooves down onto the backs of the other team.

"Whoa, easy," shouted Reuben, but he could not control Harley's rig, and as the horses jumped and kicked, the wagon tipped, losing all its load. Turning sharply, the Chupp team galloped with the empty wagon toward the other side of the field, knocking over sheaves as they went.

"Jump, Harley," Reuben yelled. "Hurry and jump off." Reuben figured it would be better if Harley would jump and perhaps sustain minor injuries than to stay with a runaway team.

Harley did jump and rolled over several times. But then to Reuben's relief, he got to his feet and managed to limp a few steps in Reuben's direction.

After such a run, Reuben had a hard time gentling his team. But once the train and the runaway horses were out of sight, he succeeded in getting them calmed down.

"Are you hurt, Harley?" Reuben asked, making his way across to where he stood, brushing dust from his clothes.

Harley had a strange expression on his face and kept looking beyond the tracks. It was almost as though his gaze was fixed on someone or something on the other side of the crossing.

Reuben repeated, "Are you hurt, Harley?"

"My ankle hurts when I put weight on it. But that's all, I think."

"Well, here, let me help you up onto the wagon. Maybe you'd better go back to the house with the water girl and get that ankle wrapped."

"Ya, I guess I'd better do that. Someone else will have to get our team."

"Here she comes now," said Reuben.

The water girl today was Harley's younger sister, Rhoda. Her job each day was to make several rounds through the field with a milk can of cold water or lemonade.

When threshing time was at Adam Weaver's, Lizzie Mae had the privilege of being water girl. Each girl felt important to be trusted to drive the family horse and buggy and perform this service.

Rhoda was alarmed to hear about the near tragedy at the crossing. She and Reuben helped Harley into her buggy, and then she stopped at each clump of men and handed them a dipper and tin cup. One dipper and one cup was shared, but the drink tasted fit for a king to the hot, thirsty, and dusty men.

The men had gathered with the boys to find out what happened. The runaway team had finally stopped in the shade of a tree at the edge of the field. Someone had fetched the rig, and the men were inspecting the wagon and horses for any damages.

Several spokes were broken from a wheel, and the breeching from one harness was torn. That was about the extent of it.

"*Was hot gewwe* (what happened)?" asked Joel Kuhn.

"Nate tried to get me to beat the train at the crossing," Harley told them.

"What!" exclaimed Atlee Kaufman. "Don't you know you could have been killed? Why, that train could never have stopped in time."

"And just what did you think *you* were doing, Reuben?"

"I had to stop Harley. I couldn't let him put himself in danger like that."

"Well, you put yourself in great danger, too. But then the Bible does say, 'Greater love hath no man than this, that a man lay down his life for his friends.' You put your life in jeopardy for Harley. We're all glad you saved his life."

Reuben was embarrassed. He didn't want such attention.

"From now on, Reuben, I'm your friend," said Harley.

"That goes for me, too," remarked Simeon. "And you sure proved you know how to handle horses."

Nate looked the other way. For once in his life he felt defeated.

25
Peace at Last

"Reuben," said Harley Chupp several weeks after his near-tragic experience with the runaway team. "Reuben, I must talk with you alone."

It was after Sunday services, and the boys already had the light lunch provided for those who cared to stay. A group had gathered under shade trees on the lawn discussing ball games, wrestling, and various other subjects.

"Where do you think we should go?" Reuben asked, mystified. He wondered why Harley wanted to see him alone.

"The buggy shed may be a good place," Harley suggested.

"Ya," Reuben agreed. "We aren't likely to be disturbed there as we would be in the barn."

"That's what I figured, too. A lot of little boys play there," Harley said.

Both boys hoped they could slip away from their

peers without being noticed. Soon their chance came. Jonas Noah's Sam started to tell about how Elam Mast bested Laban Swartz at wrestling. Sam was an Eash, and since there were three Noah Eashes on the same mail delivery route, nicknames or dad's or granddad's names were used to distinguish them.

"*Buwe* (boys)," Sam held forth, "Elam had Laban pinned before the counter said go." The counter was the referee for the wrestling match.

"Yes sir," he continued, "that little Laban got up, and he was so *verhuddelt* (mixed up), he started wrestling the counter. He always did crow a lot. He thought he could take on any boy and whip him. Bet he won't crow now. Maybe not even cackle."

This caused a bout of rousing laughter that provided the cover for Reuben and Harley to leave for the shed. It was cool and quiet inside, and except for a small gaggle of geese, they were alone. The geese hissed as though annoyed at the intrusion.

"We'll stay here by the east side, as far away from those geese as possible. I wouldn't want them setting up a racket," said Harley.

Reuben agreed. It seemed to him that Harley was stalling, working up courage to speak his mind about something.

"What is it you want to talk about, Harley?" Reuben asked. He didn't want to delay too long, lest someone come looking for them. Reuben was confident that they were alone and glad that his sister Salome no longer spied on him. Since the accident with Willy, Reuben and Salome had grown very close.

Harley cleared his throat. "Well," he began, "Reuben, it's hard for me to talk about this. I just hope you won't make *Schpott* (fun) of me. Maybe you'll understand."

Harley said no more but looked down at the floor of the buggy shed.

"Harley, I won't make *Schpott*, and I'll try to understand. What is it? You can tell me."

"It's about the many times I agreed with Nate and Simeon in calling you names and trying to get you into trouble. Then, after all that, you saved my life when I was so foolish as to take Nate's dare. Why did you do it?"

"Harley, I had to. I saw the danger you were in, and I had to stop you. I don't hold those times against you when you stuck by Nate and some others. I shouldn't have let it get to me."

"Well, I'm not going along with such actions anymore. But, Reuben, there's more I have to say. Although my dad is different since Willy is gone, he doesn't believe what I'm going to tell you. But, Reuben, it's true—I saw him. I know I did. That day in the wheat field when I tried to beat the two-forty-five, on the other side of the tracks—I saw him plain as can be!"

Harley was almost frantic now, and Reuben was puzzled.

"Saw who, Harley?" Reuben asked. "Who are you talking about?"

Now Harley's voice dropped to a near whisper. "*Willy*. Reuben, I saw Willy. He looked so nice and happy, but he was waving for me to stop. Reuben, I seemed to freeze. I wanted to stop, but I couldn't. Not until you pulled in front of my runaway horses. My family doesn't seem to believe me, but I think maybe Mom does.

"Reuben, it's true. Later, on the way home with Rhoda, I looked at the very place Willy stood, but he was gone.

"Reuben, Willy looked so wonderful. He was like a guardian angel for me that day. I've been thinking a lot the last several weeks. This fall I intend to join the church and live a different life. I've stopped running with the outback boys, and I'm trying to live for the Lord."

There! He had told Reuben everything, hoping that he would understand.

"Willy?" Reuben asked. "You saw Willy? What do you mean?"

"You don't believe it either, do you?" Harley asked, in a low tone.

"Yes, I do, Harley. You wouldn't be so sincere if it weren't true. The Bible even tells about God giving people visions. And what advantage would there be for you to make up such a story? I believe you, and I'm glad you're planning to join church this fall, for so am I. We'll be in the same group for instruction."

"Oh, really?" Harley exclaimed, with a grin. "Then we really are buddies."

Reuben saw how pleased Harley was. He decided it was about time for him to share some confidences of his own.

"Now I have something to tell you, Harley. Ever since the accident involving your brother, I have not had a moment's peace. I've blamed myself thousands of times. There were days when I wanted to get rid of my horse, Princess, and you know how much I think of her.

"Dad has told me that perhaps I took pride in that horse, and that's wrong for me to do. He also said it was not Princess's fault that the tragedy occurred. I know he's right, but oh, if it just wouldn't have happened. I've asked God to forgive me, but—how do your folks feel toward me? I must know."

"They don't blame you, and I don't, either," Harley assured him.

"Well, I'm thankful for that," Reuben murmured. "I can't forget what happened to Willy, and I wish it hadn't. But if your family isn't holding it against me, I'll try to forgive myself, too."

"Ach, Reuben, please do. Anyhow, you saved my life, and my parents will never forget that."

Reuben brushed a tear from his eye. "Thanks, Harley."

As they strolled out of the buggy shed toward the other boys, Harley asked, "Do you suppose we'll be called names if we join the church?"

"Ya, but it doesn't matter. I think there'll always be some who're wild."

"I'm glad we had this talk, and I know I feel better."

"So do I, Harley, so do I," Reuben agreed.

Some time later the bishop announced in church who was in the class of preparation for baptism. It was a surprise to many when the applicants for church membership included not only Reuben Weaver and Harley Chupp, but also Simeon Mullet and even Nate Wagler.

Perhaps Willy Chupp's death and the near-tragic accident

of his brother, Harley, were not in vain, Reuben thought. After all, the bishop often said in his sermons, "How many times good can come out of evil!"

After that service, Reuben asked Harley's permission to tell his parents about their private talk. "They'll understand," he assured him.

"Ya, go ahead," responded Harley. "And I hope we can always be friends."

"We will," said Reuben. "We're friends for life."

And finally Reuben felt at peace.

The Author

Mary Christner Borntrager of North Canton, Ohio, was raised in an Amish family of ten. According to Amish custom, her schooling was considered complete with eight grades. In later years, Mary attended teacher-training institute at Eastern Mennonite College, Harrisonburg, Virginia. She taught at a Christian day school for seven years.

After her children were grown, Mary earned a certificate in childcare and youth social work from the University of Wisconsin. For twelve years, she and her late husband, John, worked with neglected and emotionally disturbed youth.

Mary loves to write poetry and novels. She is a member of the Ohioana Library Association. A local television station and many other groups have invited her to tell about Ellie's People, her series of books,

Ellie, Rebecca, Rachel, Daniel, and *Reuben.* A young writers' convention gave her an opportunity to speak to 150 junior-high students and review their compositions.

Involvement with the extended church family means much to Mary. She is a member of the Hartville Mennonite congregation, where she is a substitute Sunday school teacher and has carried various responsibilities. Her hobbies include Bible memory, quilting, embroidery work, and word puzzles.

Mary is grateful for the many opportunities to share her faith and joy in living.